Natalie Honeycutt and her children live in San Francisco, California. INVISIBLE LISSA is her first book.

NATALIE HONEYCUTT

AN AVON CAMELOT BOOK

AVON BOOKS
A division of
The Hearst Corporation
1790 Broadway
New York, New York 10019

The Bradbury Press edition contains the following Library of Con-
gress Cataloging in Publication Data:

Honeycutt, Natalie.
   Invisible Lissa.

   Summary: Lissa badly wants to get into Debra's exclusive fifth-
grade lunch club, until she finds out what it is really like.
1. Children's stories, American. [1. Clubs—Fiction. 2. Schools—
Fiction] I. Title.
PZ7.H7467In   1985   [Fic]   84-20466

First Camelot Printing: August 1986

For
JENNIE and ANDREW,
my sources of joy

1

NEXT YEAR I'm not giving Valentine's cards to anyone. It's a big waste of time. In the first place, I don't get all that much allowance, and it took most of my allowance for the week just to get a box of twenty cards. Then that wasn't enough, because there are twenty-seven kids in my class, and I always give a card to everyone. So I had to make the rest myself. Including the card I made for Mr. Shipley, our fifth-grade teacher, and the ones for my mom and dad and my brother, that was thirty-one Valentine's cards altogether.

I got a grand total of eight cards.

Not that I've ever been the most popular girl in our class, but eight Valentine's cards? I feel like I'm slowly becoming invisible. It definitely wasn't worth all that effort. Except, that is, for the card I made for Katie.

Katie Hutchinson is my best friend. She's been taking gymnastics ever since I can remember, and she's getting really good. Twice a week her mother drives her into San Francisco for lessons, which is about thirty miles north of where we live in Westmont, California. So I made Katie a card with a drawing of a girl on a balance beam doing a handstand. She loved it.

Katie made me a card shaped like a shovel that hinged open at the top. That sounds weird, but it was actually very appropriate because, as Katie knows, I'm planning to be an archaeologist when I grow up.

I'm sure that Debra Dobbins got a card from every kid in the class. There's nothing invisible about her. Debra only came to Jefferson School in the middle of last year when her family moved here from Chicago, and by the end of the year she was probably the best-liked girl in the class. She even got invited to Sherry Eisenberg's birthday party, and I've known Sherry since first grade and she never invited me.

Even the people who weren't too sure about Debra at first ended up trying to be friends with her. Including me, I have to admit. I was always complimenting her on her clothes and hair and stuff, which is easy because her parents must buy her a new outfit once a week, and her hair always looks like she'd just had it professionally styled. She looks like an ad for The Perfect Child. Plus she's enthusiastic, short and bouncy, and full of ideas. Debra was nice to me at first, too, especially when I was complimenting her. But lately she mostly ignores me. I even loaned her my four-color pen the day after I got it, and she never gave it back.

Maybe it's because she ignores me, or maybe because

2

I'm annoyed about my pen, but Debra Dobbins is starting to give me a real pain.

On the morning of Valentine's Day, Katie and I got to school early. We were the Decorating Committee for the class party, and we hung chains of red hearts from the light fixtures, then twisted red and white streamers around the blackboard and over the doors and windows. It looked pretty great, if I say so myself.

We were finished a few minutes before the bell rang, so there was still time left over to deliver our cards before everyone else came in. Usually you have to sneak them into people's desks and backpacks during the day, which is tricky, since everyone else is doing the same thing.

As soon as the bell rang, everyone gathered on the floor in the clear space in front of Mr. Shipley's desk for Morning Meeting. Mr. Shipley checked the attendance, and then, just as he was about to start announcements, Debra came running in late. She squeezed in between Tina Chin and Sherry. Tina and Sherry used to be best friends, but now they're both sort of Debra's best friend.

Right away Debra caused a sensation. She was wearing red ribbons in her hair, red shoes, white tights and a dress with little hearts and cupids all over it, edged in lace. It was really a spectacular outfit—though if I'd known she was going to come to school dressed as a Valentine, Katie and I could have skipped the decorations.

"Okay," Mr. Shipley said. "Let's settle down now... okay?" The girls were all making a lot of racket telling Debra how beautiful she looked. And even a couple of boys who hardly ever say anything were saying, "Hi, Debra..."

"Does anyone hear me?" Mr. Shipley asked. "Last call. We have a lot of work to get accomplished before our party today," he said.

"Awww..." came the protests.

"And I know you're all going to cooperate so we can begin the party on *time*, right?" He beamed one of his big smiles around at us, and everyone quieted down.

Mr. Shipley's very young for a teacher, and a lot of the girls think he looks like a movie star with his gleaming teeth and curly hair. I haven't decided yet whether he does or not, but I do know Mr. Shipley always tries to be fair.

The thing is, though, that I think sometimes he tries *too* hard. He can end up missing the most obvious things. Like when he put up a chart for classroom chores at the beginning of the year. He said he didn't want to assign chores because it seemed too "regimented" to him. And he thought that since some people like certain chores more than others, it would make more sense if we picked our own. So we all just signed up for whichever job we wanted.

That was dandy, except that it took him until the end of November to notice that about five kids had never signed up for anything, and the rest of us were doing their share of the work.

Mr. Shipley made an announcement about Lost and Found—that we should all go and check because the school secretary was being forced out of her office for lack of space. Next he reminded a couple of people about overdue homework. Then, just as he was saying, "Well, that about wraps it up..." Debra started waving her hand and talking.

"Ohhh...Mr. Shipley...wait! I have a special announcement." She stood up and smoothed down the front of her skirt while everyone waited.

"It's a surprise," she continued. "A special surprise for our teacher. Let me have it, Tina." Tina handed up a plastic bag, and Debra pulled out a heart-shaped box of candy. A big one. It must have been the five-pound size.

"This is a gift in honor of our teacher," she said, presenting the box to Mr. Shipley. "It's because you're the best fifth-grade teacher ever."

I thought Mr. Shipley looked slightly uncomfortable, but he beamed another of his smiles and said, "Why, thank you, Debra. That's very sweet—if you'll excuse the pun." Debra was radiant.

"It's from all three of us," Sherry spoke up.

"Oh, yes," Debra said. "It's from Sherry and Tina, too. But *I'm* making the presentation, since it was my idea and all."

"Well, thank you, all," Mr. Shipley said, and some of the kids started to murmur about what a nice idea it was to give Mr. Shipley a box of candy.

"Hey," Zack Brady said, "that's *bribery.*" You can always count on Zack to say exactly what he thinks, which is one of the reasons not too many people like him. But sometimes I secretly admire him for it.

"You're not supposed to bribe a teacher," Zack said. "In the first place, bribery is illegal. I know that for a fact. Plus, my mother says it's in poor taste."

"It's *not* bribery," Debra said. "It's a *present*. There's a difference, you know."

"That's right," Tina said. "It's just a present. There's nothing wrong with presents."

Mr. Shipley cut in. "I'm sure no one would object, though, if I shared this box of candy with the class..."

A chorus of "Yea..." went up, and Debra looked momentarily crushed.

"But that's not fair," she said. "Maybe we should vote." Debra doesn't give up very easily.

"It's fair to my dentist," Mr. Shipley said, grinning. Then he added, "But don't worry, I'll get my share," and patted Debra on the back.

* * *

5

I don't know who got much work accomplished that day, but I know I didn't. I kept thinking up excuses to leave my desk so there'd be plenty of opportunity for anyone to deliver Valentine's cards in case they felt like it. By one-thirty when Mr. Shipley said we could stop working and set up for the party, I'd been to the girls' room six times and the pencil sharpener seventeen times. Two nearly new pencils were down to tiny nubs.

Someone had brought in a portable stereo tape player and some rock tapes, and we shoved the desks to the sides of the room to make space for dancing. The Refreshment Committee set up a table full of cookies and cupcakes and drinks.

Mostly the girls did the dancing, though, and the boys occupied themselves with the food. I didn't dance because that's one of the things I'm really lousy at. Katie tried to teach me once, and I think I have all the basics down. But somehow when I start dancing I end up stepping on my own feet or someone else's, and then I get confused and turn at the wrong time and generally look like a jerk.

Katie danced with Rob Ganz three times. I poked her in the side and said, "I told you so," because I've been telling Katie all year that I think Rob Ganz is in love with her. He calls her on the phone sometimes, and today he even gave her a special card in a thick red envelope.

But Katie said the card had a joke, and she thinks they're just good friends—so I guess we can't say for sure.

Joel Osborne ate the most refreshments of anyone. Joel eats more than anyone I know, and since he's not especially tall you'd think he'd blow up like a balloon. But he's all bones. Bones with red hair on top. He belongs to a soccer team, the Grasshoppers, and today he was wearing his uniform, which just made his legs look all the skinnier. I was staring at him as he chomped down what must have been his third cupcake and began peeling the wrapper off a fourth. I started to wonder whether, if he ate enough cupcakes, his legs would fill out so you couldn't notice his knobby knees. Or would his knees grow while the rest of him didn't?

While I was worrying about that, Debra walked up to him and said, "You know, Joel, you really should ask a girl to dance. It's impolite not to." Meaning her, I'm sure. But Joel just turned red and said he wasn't in the mood to dance.

I could have told Debra that Joel would say that because I happen to know that he can't dance yet. Joel lives next-door to me, and I know quite a few things about him that not everyone knows. Not that I'd tell or anything, because Joel and I have always been friends. In fact, he's the closest thing I ever had to a boyfriend, if you can count your next-door neighbor.

Joel and I used to walk to school together every day, but last year some of the boys started saying I was his girlfriend, and pretty soon Joel was leaving without me some mornings. Finally one day Zack said, "Hey, when are you two getting married?" I thought Joel and I would both barf. That was last spring, and we haven't walked to school together since.

Katie thinks I'm lucky to have Joel living right across the driveway from me. But I explained to her that if you want to have a boyfriend, it's a lot better if he lives farther away.

That's the other thing I could have told Debra—that Joel isn't interested in girls yet. If he were, I'd know.

I was studying Mr. Shipley's box of candy, which he had put on the refreshment table, when Katie came back from dancing with Rob.

"I'm going to have one of these as soon as I figure out

which ones don't have nuts," I explained. I usually like nuts, but not in candy.

Katie said, "At home I just poke a little hole in the bottom to check. But if you get one with nuts, I'll eat it."

I stood there trying to decide. Finally I picked a smooth, dark brown one that was perfectly square. It turned out to be coconut, my favorite.

"If this candy was supposed to be a bribe for Mr. Shipley, I hope Debra wasn't too disappointed," I said. "All she really got for it was a pat on the back and a dance with him."

"But *she* asked *him* for the dance," Katie said.

"I know. And then he danced with Cindy, too. And Cindy didn't give him anything."

"Well—maybe Debra just wants to be special," Katie said.

I giggled. "I'm *sure* Debra wants to be special," I said. "She always does. I mean, she was probably hoping there'd be a prize for best costume today, like she got at Halloween."

Katie's eyes got big, and she started pointing with her thumb toward my stomach.

"But it seems a little impractical, don't you think?" I went on. "I mean, where else can she wear a dress with cupids and hearts all over it? She'll just have to buy something new for Fourth of July . . ."

Katie's eyes were almost bulging, and she was gesturing like mad at my stomach. I brushed my hand down my front in case I had crumbs on my shirt.

". . . and just imagine Easter," I laughed. "She'll probably get a dress with chicks and bunnies hopping all around." I took a little hop backward to demonstrate— and bumped right into someone.

"Oh, sorry," I said, turning around.

8

It was Debra. She had her hands on her hips and was glaring at me.

"*Watch* it, Lissa," she said.

"Debra...I...uh..." My voice croaked. "Hi," I said.

Debra didn't answer. She just stayed there glaring.

I was stuck. There was no way to tell for sure if she'd heard me. Then again, I didn't want to start apologizing in case she hadn't. My mind raced, trying to think of something offhand to say.

"These are really good candies," I pronounced, reaching for another. I took a bite. It had nuts, but I just chewed and smiled. "*Really* good," I said.

"I didn't get them for *you*, Lissa," she said.

I swallowed.

"And by the way," she said, "I've been meaning to ask you, can't your parents afford to buy you new shoes?"

I looked down at my shoes. A torn Velcro fastener was dangling from one, and the sole was flapping loose on the front of the other. Considering that my mother had bought them for me just three weeks ago, they were pretty beat-up.

"But they *are* new..." I began. Only Debra had walked away.

"I *tried* to tell you," Katie said.

I moaned. Suddenly my stomach hurt. Maybe I'm allergic to nuts, I thought.

"Do you think she heard?" I asked. "I mean, Debra's not the sort of person you'd want for an enemy."

"I don't know. I *thought* she heard, but now I don't know." Katie looked thoughtful for a minute. "I guess you'll find out, though," she said.

That's just what I *didn't* want—to find out. My stomach clenched into a tight fist, and I started to wonder if the party was ever going to be over.

At five minutes before the bell, I took one last look

9

through my desk, just in case any more cards had arrived since I'd last checked. None had. Then I headed for the girls' coatroom to collect my junk. As usual, the coatroom was clogged up with backpacks all over the floor and a sleeping bag or two. I made it to my jacket, then wiggled into my backpack and headed for the door.

That's when I found it. The card that brought my grand total to eight. It was stuffed in my jacket pocket.

For some stupid reason I felt a little burst of "Oh, goodie" as I yanked it out of my pocket. Then I looked at it.

"TO LISA W.," it said on the envelope.

That creep. She still can't spell my name. There's only one kid in the class who misspells my name: Bernice Wilkins, the world's biggest drip. She's the only girl who still wears her hair in braids. And if it looks like it might rain even a drop, she wears boots to school. Which is doubly ridiculous because when it does rain, her mother always drives her. Personally, I'd like to see Bernice get soaking wet some day.

The least she could do is learn to spell my name right. It's Lissa, not Lisa. Short for Melissa Woodbury. Five years in the same class, and she still can't spell my name.

As the bell rang, I crumpled the card in my hand and dropped it in the wastebasket on my way out the door.

2

"JASON, BE QUIET. I'm trying to sleep."

"I *am* being quiet, Lissa."

"Singing in a high, squeaky voice is not being quiet, Jason, so kindly pipe down." That's one of the disadvantages of sharing your room with your little brother: you can't sleep late on weekends. There are about fifty other disadvantages, and I'm keeping a list. I'll add this to it—disadvantage number fifty-one. I turned on my side and smashed my ears between the pillow and my stuffed rabbit.

"But I was singing *quietly*. I can sing louder, you know."

I didn't respond. Maybe if I just acted like I'd gone back to sleep he would shut up.

For a couple of minutes I thought it had worked. Then

11

I felt warm breath on my face. Jason breath. I opened one eye, and there he was, about three inches from my face, staring at me with his dopey, lopsided grin. I couldn't help it, I started to laugh.

"Ha!" Jason said. "You weren't really sleeping. You were just hiding under your rabbit!"

"Jason, you're hopeless," I said.

"Know what day this is, Lissa?"

"I know, Squirt. It's Saturday."

"It's Saturday, Lissa."

"I know, Jason."

"And it's a stay-home day. You stay home from school, and I stay home from kindergarten and the sitter, and Daddy stays home from work and Mommy stays home from work."

"I *know*, Jason. Didn't I just say I know?" Really, I shouldn't bother. Once Jason gets started, he's nearly impossible to stop.

"Want me to sing you my song, Lissa? It's about me."

"No thanks," I said. Not to be mean, but I knew he'd do it anyway, so it didn't matter what I said.

"It goes like this," he said, and he swung his arms and hips around as he sang at the top of his voice:

> "*John* Jason *Jingleheimer Smith,*
> *That's my name, too.*
> *Whenever I go out, the people always shout,*
> *It's John* Jason *Jingleheimer Smith!*"

As he finished, he flung himself on the floor, spread-eagled, for emphasis.

"Did you like it?" he asked. "Don't I sing good songs?"

"It was great, Jason. Truly unique." And it *was* unique, too. Not only because he'd fudged the words to get his name in, but he doesn't carry a tune very well yet, and his speech is barely intelligible. I can understand him fine, and so do my parents, but otherwise, unless you've spent a lot of time with him, you'd need a translator.

For ages, I kept telling Mom and Dad there was something wrong with the way Jason talked, and that they should do something. I'd been trying since Jason was two years old to get him to say my name right, but it always came out "Witha." Even when I offered him gum as a reward, he still couldn't do it. But naturally my parents wouldn't listen to my advice about Jason. They never do.

Then Jason's kindergarten teacher phoned and said she thought Jason should see a speech therapist. They listened to *her*. They had Jason tested and signed up at a speech clinic within twenty-four hours. It was probably some sort of record.

So far it hasn't exactly transformed his speech. He's only learned one sound: *s*. But now he says my name "Wissa," instead of "Witha," and that's progress.

"When does Jason get a new sound?" I asked at breakfast. Mom and Dad and I were having French toast, but Jason was eating Kix. It's the only thing he'll eat for breakfast.

"His therapist said maybe next week," Mom answered.

"Oh, good. Could you ask them to give him *l* next? I can't wait to hear what it sounds like when he can say my name right."

"You'll just have to be patient, Lissa," Mom said. "They do the sounds in a special order, and I think *sh* is next."

"Well, ask anyway, okay? Just in case?"

After breakfast Dad announced he was going to the art supply store and to the hardware store, and would anyone like to go with him? That was our cue; Jason and I both said we wanted to. I said it because I know Mom tries to catch up on the housework on Saturdays, and if I hang around she puts me to work. Jason just likes to go places, so he'd say yes anyway.

My dad's an artist, which is the main reason I have to share my room with Jason—Dad uses the third bedroom as an art studio. I think it's a waste of space, because he only uses it on weekends. He says it's hard to make a living as a painter if you live near San Francisco because every third person has the same idea. So on weekdays he works in the city, doing commercial art for a magazine. But he keeps hoping that some day he can sell the paintings he does on weekends, and maybe eventually he'll even get rich and famous. The thing is, he's been saying that for years. So I don't think I ought to count on it.

"Could we go to the library, too, Dad?" I asked. "All of my books are due."

I usually check out my books from the Westmont Public Library because I don't like to go to the school library. Mrs. Ivers, the school librarian, has a glass eye, and lots of kids say she's really a witch. All I know is it's weird to try to talk to her, because you can never figure out which eye she can see out of.

"Sure, if you just drop them off," he answered. "But I won't have time to wait if you want to browse. So you might want to go on your bike instead."

"No, that's okay," I said, "I'll just drop them off."

We went to the hardware store first, and by the time we got to the library I had changed my mind about wanting to browse. While we were in Billings Hardware, Dad had stuck me with watching Jason, and after forty-five minutes of hauling him away from bins of light switches, nails and pipe joints, I was ready for a break. I told Dad I wanted to find some books to check out, and that I'd walk home later.

I got a book about a girl who becomes a marathon runner, and one about a bunch of kids who explore caves and

14

three volumes of *Two Minute Mysteries*. I'm getting hooked on those mysteries; sometimes you can figure them out before the end if you pay attention to details that don't quite fit.

On the way home I took a "shortcut" and went through Hanley Park. It's actually four blocks out of my way, but I wanted to stop by the creek which runs through the north side of the park.

I'm not supposed to go to the creek without my parents' permission, especially in the rainy season. Just mentioning the creek is enough to freak my mother out. She's convinced I'll drown.

Actually, you *could* drown there during a heavy rainstorm. Sometimes the water gets all the way to the top of the bank and really roars by. When you see it carrying away huge branches, you realize you wouldn't stand a chance if you fell in. So when I go, I always stay at a respectful distance. One thing even worse than drowning would be to have your mother mad at you for it.

Today, though, the water was low, not more than a couple of feet deep. So I squeezed through the gap in the chain-link fence and found a clear space to sit on the bank.

I like to imagine what it must have been like here a couple of hundred years ago, before the chain-link fence on the park side, and before the houses and their backyard fences on the other bank. There would have been fields and dense brush, stands of trees and tons of wild animals. Thousands and thousands of birds, and deer, and rabbits and even bears. And there would have been Indians... definitely Indians.

Joel and I found out about the Indians while we were exploring the creek last summer. The creekbed was dry then, and we were using sticks to dig out steps on the side of the bank so it wouldn't be so hard to get back up all the time. While we were digging, we kept digging out

15

shells, so we made collections of them and took a bunch home.

One afternoon when my dad came home from work, we had the shells spread all over the back steps.

"What's all this?" he said.

I thought he was about to lecture us on leaving things where people could trip on them, so I said, "Just shells," and started to gather them up.

"I can see that," he said, "but where did you get them?"

"From the creek," Joel said, and explained about the steps we were digging.

"That's extraordinary," said Dad. "You must be digging into a shell mound!"

"What's a shell mound?" Neither of us had ever heard of one.

Then Dad told us that years ago Indians used to live all around this area, before Westmont was even here, and before California was even California. He said that one of the things they ate the most was shellfish—clams and oysters and mussels—from the Bay, and that piles of shells were left where their villages used to be. He said that over the years the shell mounds got pretty deep, some as much as ten or twenty feet.

"Wow." You could see Joel was impressed. "You mean Indians used to live by the creek?"

"Well, if you're finding that many shells mixed with the soil by the creek," Dad said, "it's the only explanation I can think of. Oysters only live in saltwater, so if you're finding oyster shells by a freshwater creek, they must have been carried there from the Bay."

I was trying to picture it—these enormous piles of shells with Indians living on top. "But I don't get it," I said. "Do you mean the Indians actually lived *on* the shells? Wouldn't that be like living at the town dump?"

My father laughed. I hate it when he laughs when I ask

16

a perfectly logical question. "I doubt it was like living at the dump, Lissa. We're talking about hundreds of thousands of years, and a lot of soil mixed in. Shells aren't the same as tin cans, you know. Anyhow, I don't honestly know *how* the Indians lived. So if you want to know more, you'll have to ask someone else."

After that, Joel and I forgot all about the steps and just started excavating big holes in the banks of the creek. We brought home sacks full of shells and sorted them into piles along the fence by the lemon tree. Finally I started to get really curious about the Indians, and eventually I went to the public library and asked whether they had any books about the local Indians.

It turned out that there were only three books about them, and even the librarian had a hard time finding them. They hadn't been checked out in years, and it seemed like everyone had forgotten all about the Indians except me and Joel.

The Indians were called the Ohlones, and they were really neat. They had a happy and well organized way of living, and they were experts at getting along with each other. In fact, they might have held some sort of record for living in peace. Some people think they lived here for more than five thousand years without any major wars. When you consider that we've only been living here for a couple of hundred years and we've had lots of wars, it might have been better if the Ohlones had been allowed to run things.

The sad part, though, is that they're dead. Almost every single one of them. And what mostly killed them was germs, ordinary germs.

When the Spanish came here from the south they rounded up the Indians and made them go live in missions, so they could teach them how to be "civilized" and turn them all into Christians. But pretty soon the Indians started catching diseases from the missionaries, and then they started dying, by the hundreds and then by the thousands. There weren't many left by the time the American settlers got here, but the Americans starved or murdered most of the rest of the Indians.

After reading that, I decided I want to be an archaeologist when I grow up. So I can help find out about people who might otherwise be forgotten—like the Ohlone Indians, who are gone for good.

I stayed longer than I meant to by the creek, but nobody said anything about it when I got home. Dad and Jason were already back, and Dad was in an uproar because Jason had rearranged half the art supply store while Dad was busy choosing a brush.

"I don't know how he did it so *fast*," Dad was saying. "He put cadmium yellow pales in with cadmium yellow deeps, and lamp blacks in with ivory blacks, and raw umbers in with burnt umbers... all apparently because he thought it made more sense to have exactly the same number of tubes of paint in each box. Then, while I was getting *that* sorted out, Jason was reorganizing all the felt-tipped pens on the other side of the aisle. I thought we'd never get out of there."

Poor Dad, he looked really frazzled. And Mom didn't act too sympathetic. She said Jason does the same thing when she takes him to the grocery store.

"You know," I said helpfully, "they make these things to put on little kids. They fasten on over the chest like a harness and zip up the back. And there's this long rope attached. It works just like a leash..."

"*Lissa!*" Mom and Dad said in unsion.

I don't know why they had to sound so shocked. A leash is just what Jason needs. Honestly, my parents never take my advice. I don't know why I waste my breath.

3

"Is your yogurt spoiled or sour or something?" Katie asked.

We were eating our lunches outside the classrooms, on the benches along the edge of the blacktop. Which you can do if it's not raining, and if you bring your own lunch. This Tuesday was one of those warm, hazy February days that feels like late May. I always bring my lunch, since Mom says it's uneconomical to eat in the cafeteria. And since I also have to *make* my own lunch, it's usually either a peanut-butter-and-jelly sandwich or yogurt. Mostly I bring yogurt. It's quicker.

"No," I said. "Why'd you ask that?"

"Because you were making a pruney face."

"So would you if you were thinking about Mr. Shipley."

"I *like* Mr. Shipley," Katie protested.

"Oh, so do I. But I'm going to stop liking him if he doesn't quit giving us these yucky projects to do."

"Oh, that." Katie took another bite out of her sandwich. "That's not so bad. I mean I suppose there are worse things to do than a project on our city. And he said we could choose almost anything so long as it really had to do with the topic."

"'What Makes Westmont Run—Our Government, Our People, Our Resources,'" I quoted. "Ick."

"Well, I think I'm going to do mine on trees. I have a book at home called *The Trees of Westmont*, and my mother's on the Beautification Commission, so I should be able to get a lot of help from her."

"You're amazing," I said. "It takes me ages to think of something to do, and then I usually come up with a dumb idea. Like that project I did last fall on Greek and Roman fashions."

"Oh, but that was a perfectly good idea..." Katie began. Then she started to giggle. "It was just the... the way it came out."

"That's okay, you can laugh. It's just that I can't draw people face-front, you know..."

It did sort of seem funny now, but I sure didn't think it was funny at the time. It took me forever just to come up with the idea of "fashions" for our Greek and Roman project. Then I got really involved in it and did a lot of research and drew all these pictures of different things people wore at different times. But since I couldn't make the noses come out right from the front, I ended up drawing all the people in profile.

That was okay, only I was so worried about the noses I never stopped to think about the breasts. It wasn't until people started laughing in class while I was explaining my posters that I caught on. Without thinking, I had made all

20

the women with too-large breasts that stood straight out. They looked absurd, and most people seemed to think I'd done it on purpose. I was mortified.

"Look," Katie said, "he said we could do our projects in pairs, so do you want to do trees with me?"

"Oh . . . I don't know, Katie. I mean, no offense or anything, but I guess I'm not all that interested in trees."

"Yeah, I guess trees are sort of dull . . . But look at it this way," she said, suddenly snickering, "at least trees don't have breasts."

I hooted, and Katie completely cracked up laughing.

"Oh, and look what you did," Katie gasped. "Your shirt's a wreck."

"Oh, no!" I had sputtered yogurt all down the front of my cream-colored shirt. "And it's *blueberry*," I wailed. "Why did it have to be blueberry? My mother's going to kill me."

"Yeah, Lissa. Really. You should have brought lemon. It would have been more discreet."

"It's not funny," I said, trying hard not to laugh. "I have to get this cleaned up. Please, I mean it. You have to stop laughing."

"I will," she roared. "Honest, I will. Soon. I hope."

We used up about a ton of paper towels and about half the soap in the dispenser trying to get my shirt clean. The stain got lighter, which was good. But it also got bigger, which wasn't so good. Plus I got a sudsy feeling inside my shirt from all the soap that got through. I had an idea that from now on this was going to be one of those shirts that could only be worn under another shirt.

We gave up and headed back outside just in time to practically collide with Bernice. She was all excited and red in the face from running.

"Oh, there you are," she panted. "I've been looking all over for you."

"Whatever for?" I asked sarcastically. I couldn't help it; Bernice always brings out the worst in me.

"There's a meeting. At the tree stump outside the cafeteria. And you're supposed to come quick."

"What meeting?" Katie asked.

"It's for Debra," Bernice answered breathlessly. "She's going to make an announcement to all the fifth-grade girls. So you have to be there. And," she went on, drawing herself up proudly, "Debra picked *me* to tell everyone."

That figures, I thought. Leave it to Bernice to think it was a big honor to run around and get all sweaty delivering Debra's messages for her.

Katie and I were the last to arrive, and Debra was standing on the step, already talking.

"... so it seems like maybe they just need someone to cheer for them. I mean, the Grasshoppers would be a pretty good team if they could just win some games. So I have this idea that if we organized some cheerleaders we could go cheer for them and maybe they'd win. See?"

"Oh, neat," Sherry said right away. "That's a great idea, Debra. I'll cheer with you."

"Yeah. Me, too. Oh, super..." a bunch of other people chimed in quickly.

"Oh, but *wait*," Debra said. "I mean it has to be *real* cheerleaders. Everyone has to try out first. Except for me, that is. Since it was my idea and all. There'll be five cheerleaders altogether, including me. And anyone who wants can try out. That's what this announcement is for—to say tryouts are going to be at lunch recess tomorrow."

"But what are we supposed to do?"

"Who's going to be the judge for us?"

"If you'd just *wait* a minute, I'm going to show you," Debra said. "I'm going to show everyone a cheer, and then you can practice it. And whoever does it best will get chosen. Oh... and *I'm* going to do the choosing, of course.

I mean, I think that's the most fair, don't you, since I thought of it and all?"

Nobody disagreed. But then, nobody ever does disagree with Debra. Everyone joined in right away and started learning the cheer with her. Including me and Katie. It wasn't all that hard, since it was only four lines long. But it had a catch—it ended with a cartwheel and then a leap in the air.

That was going to eliminate a lot of people right there. A cartwheel is just one of those things that not everyone can do. I hadn't done one myself for about two years, and I wasn't sure I could manage it. Bernice started to whine about how impossible it was, but Debra told her, "Just practice, you'll get it," and Bernice shut up.

"Are you going to try out?" Katie asked.

"I don't know. *You* should, though. You're great. It must be all that gymnastics training."

"Yeah, well I will if you will."

"Oh, Katie. Coordination isn't one of my biggest talents, remember?"

"Yeah, but cartwheels *are*. You used to be some sort of cartwheel freak. You did them constantly. I remember the first time you ever came over to my house, you insisted on doing cartwheels the whole way there. I thought you were really strange."

That was true. I had a real thing about cartwheels for a while. Cartwheels and headstands. I went through a phase where I was upside down almost as much as I was right side up. It nearly drove my family crackers. Every day I used to listen for my dad's car to pull in the driveway after work, then I'd dash to the front hallway and stand on my head. That way, the first thing he'd see as he came in the door was me, upside down, saying, "Hi, Dad...How was your day?" in this very casual

23

voice. He was supposed to think I'd been there all afternoon waiting for him.

"Oh, come on, Lissa. Say you'll do it. It'll be much more
fun if we both try out."

"All right," I said. "I'll do it. But if I make a fool of
myself I'm going to blame you."

"Don't worry, you won't. Just practice and you'll be
good. Trust me.

"Oh, but, Lissa," she added, "just one thing: I think
maybe you should wear a clean shirt."

"Scum," I said, and swatted her.

I started practicing in the back yard as soon as I got
home. Though it wasn't easy with Jason underfoot. He
had the whole thing memorized in about five minutes and
kept trying to join in.

"Jason," I said, finally, "you're really messing me up.
Could you just sit down for a while and watch instead?"

"But I'm going to be a cheerleader, too," he said.

"No you're not, Squirt."

"But why, Lissa?"

"Because you're not old enough yet. And it's for girls.
And you have to be able to do a cartwheel. And about five
other reasons. So could you stay out of my way?"

He sat down, dejectedly, and I started over. It wasn't
all that hard once you got the hang of it, and pretty soon
I concentrated on trying to get my leaps extra high and
perfecting my cartwheel.

"Lissa?" Jason was right in front of me again.

"Oh, Jason, *what?* You're being a certified pain, you
know."

"I know," he sighed. "But, Lissa? Could you teach me
a cartwheel? Then I could be a cheerleader, too."

"Oh, I give up, Jason. Okay, I'll teach you. But you still

can't be a cheerleader. And then you have to *promise* to stay out of my way, you hear?"

"I will, Lissa."

Things improved after that. Jason stayed out of my way and just practiced his cartwheels. They didn't even remotely resemble real cartwheels, though, because he nearly destroyed himself the first few times by whomping over on his back. So he invented a safer version where he just put both palms flat on the ground and hopped up a little with his feet. But it didn't seem to bother him, that he couldn't do the real thing. He was blissfully proud of himself.

When Dad came home, Jason insisted on showing him his cartwheel act.

"Hey, terrific, Jason," Dad said, clapping. "Take a bow, kid." Jason took a couple of bows. Then he did more cartwheels and took a few more bows. Dad thought it was hysterical and kept clapping and laughing and egging Jason on.

"Now I'm a cartwheel *hero*, right, Daddy?"

"Right, Jason!"

"And I can be a cheerleader, too! Right, Daddy?"

"Right, Jason!"

"Dad," I said in my most exasperated voice, "you're going to warp that kid if you keep telling him a bunch of junk that isn't true. How do you ever expect him to learn anything?"

Dad just pretended he didn't hear me. Parents can be so dumb.

Word must have gotten around fast about the cheerleader tryouts, because at lunch recess the next day the whole fifth grade was there, girls and boys. Plus a few other kids, besides. That made me nervous. If I was going to make a fool of myself, I would have preferred a smaller crowd.

25

The boys who were on the soccer team seemed to think it was a neat idea. Although Rob did say maybe some people would object, since the Grasshoppers were an American Soccer League team, not just a team from our school. Anyone in Westmont could be on it if they tried out.

"I don't think anyone will care," Joel said. "After all, there are only three guys on the team who aren't in our class. And only one of them is actually from a different school, and I'm sure he wouldn't mind."

"Well, I think it's a harebrained idea," Zack said.

"Nobody asked you," someone yelled.

"That's the whole point," Zack said. "Nobody asked *them*. Who ever heard of an ASL soccer team that had cheerleaders, anyhow? If they're so crazy about soccer, why don't they start their own team?"

"Shut up, Zack."

"And furthermore," he went on, "my sister says it's things like cheerleaders that keep the women's movement stuck in the Dark Ages."

"Your sister's a geek," someone said.

"I know that," Zack hollered. "But at least she has some self-respect, which is more than I can say for some people."

I kind of think you have to hand it to someone who can admit his own sister is a geek. But everyone kept shouting at him until he finally gave up with, "Okay, have it your way. Act like imbeciles. Make a mockery of the whole sport of soccer. See if I care!"

Debra said that everyone who was trying out should get in a line. She had a notepad and pencil and said she would write down our names in order as we took our turns. Tina was first, since she was standing right next to Debra when she said that.

"We've got the spirit
We've got the team

26

We've got the boys who're
Right on the beam!
Go-o-o-o-o-o TEAM!"

Tina was perfect. She was even better than Debra was when she demonstrated the cheer to us. The cartwheel came on the "go-o-o" part, followed by a big leap on "TEAM!" Tina looked like she was ready for high-school cheerleading at least. She must have practiced all night.

Sherry was next, then Marla, then Cindy, then Katie, then me. I was nervous the whole time, right up to the second I started my turn. Then I was suddenly relaxed. It was the strangest sensation, like I was somebody else just calmly watching myself. My cartwheel was flawless, and I could tell I had jumped higher than ever. It was spooky.

"That was *great*," Katie whispered.

"Thanks," I said. "*You* were terrific. You were as good as Tina."

"Thanks," she said. "It's probably all those gymnastics lessons. But you were great, too. Just wait and see. I'm sure you'll be chosen."

A couple of other girls did really well, but lots of them flubbed their cartwheels on the first try and had to start over again. Even then not everybody could do one. Bernice's cartwheel was the worst, though. She looked like she'd been taking lessons from Jason.

Katie and I kept track. We figured that the four best were Tina, Katie, Cindy and me. Counting Debra, that was five.

Debra didn't announce her choices right away. When everyone had finished trying out, she went and sat down on the stump and started making little marks on her notepad, looking very intent. Everyone just stood off at a short distance watching her and sort of shifting around and acting restless. It seemed to me that she was enjoying keeping

27

everyone in suspense. After the longest time she stood up and climbed onto the stump.

"First of all," she said solemnly, "this was a very difficult decision. Everyone was so good." I don't know why she said that, since it was perfectly obvious that some people were lousy. Maybe she had rehearsed it. "It was really close," she went on, "so I hope nobody feels bad if they don't get chosen. And now... the names of the official cheerleaders for the Grasshoppers..."

"I still think you were good," Katie said later.

I shrugged. I should have known, I thought.

"Honest, Lissa, you *were* good. I know you were better than Sherry, anyhow. I don't know why Debra picked her. Sherry was one of the worst."

"Oh, Katie, don't be dense. Debra picked her because Sherry's her friend. I just should have figured she would."

"I guess you're right," Katie said. "I mean, I know that's why she picked her. But it just seems so *unfair*, you know?"

"*Katie*, wake up. That's the whole point. Debra's never fair, in case you hadn't noticed. Except to Debra, that is. She's always fair to herself."

"I just feel really bad, though. I mean I talked you into it and everything."

I realized I was being sort of mean to Katie. I didn't blame Katie, but I felt like a jerk for even trying out.

"Well, I'm glad you got in," I said. "I'm just mad at Debra. And myself. But I'll probably get over it. At least I'm pretty sure I'll get over being mad at *myself*. I'm not positive about Debra."

"That's okay," Katie said with a little giggle. "I think Debra can handle it."

"Yeah... considering she'll probably never even notice."

28

"I felt kind of sorry for Bernice, though. Did you?" Katie asked.

"I don't know. Not really, I guess. I just wish she hadn't cried. It made me feel all embarrassed. That's dumb—*she* was sitting there crying, and *I* felt embarrassed."

"I know," Katie said. "And then she begged Debra to let her be an alternate."

"I just wish she wouldn't act the way she does, you know?"

"Yeah, I know. I guess Bernice just wants to have friends, though."

"So does everyone," I said. "But Bernice sure goes about it the wrong way." Not that I'm any expert, I thought. But at least I'm not Bernice.

It seemed like all anyone could talk about for the next ten days was cheerleading. Debra held practice sessions every noontime, and Katie always gobbled her lunch so she could get there in time. Then, on the days she didn't have gymnastics lessons, she would stay after school and practice some more. Like most of the other noncheerleaders, I just hung around and watched.

After a few days it started to get on my nerves. I could see cheerleaders jumping up and down in my head every night when I closed my eyes. I started wishing I had something else to do at lunch recess. It would have to be something important, though, or Katie might feel insulted. For some reason, she seemed to take it for granted that I would find it fascinating to spend all my time watching her learn cheers.

"And guess what," she said on the fifth day. "Debra's mother is going to make us all matching skirts out of green felt. With green felt underpants attached. Isn't that neat?"

"Sure," I said. I guess so. Why not? I tried to imagine *my* mother volunteering to make cheerleading skirts for four of my friends. I couldn't. I tried to imagine her making one for just me, instead. I couldn't imagine that, either.

"And you're going to come to the game next Saturday, aren't you? Lissa, you just *have* to. It's going to be so great. Besides, I need you for moral support. I don't think I could do it if you didn't come."

"Sure," I said again. Sure I'll come. I hate soccer games. I hate team sports in general. I've never been to a game of any kind in my whole life. But I'll come. I'm too fascinated to stay home.

4

"OH, MOM," I said on Saturday, "do I have to take Jason with me? He won't understand the game, and he'll just get restless and bored. I'll end up chasing him all over instead of watching the game. It's not fair."

"Lissa, you don't even like soccer, so why don't you stay home with Jason instead?"

"But I promised Katie..."

"Then you'll *have* to take him," she said, sounding exasperated. "It's very important for your father and me to go see this gallery, and you've known for a month you were expected to babysit."

I decided not to tell her I thought the whole idea of going to the gallery was dumb. They were planning to look at a cooperative art gallery, where artists can rent space to hang up their paintings. Only it seems to me that if you have to pay to get people to look at your paintings, you're probably doing something wrong.

"All right," I said, "I'll take him. But I'm not going to like it."

"You don't have to like it," Mom said in an irritated tone, "but you do have to take good care of Jason. And I want you both to wear your rain slickers. It looks threatening."

"Aw, Mom..." I hate those yellow rain slickers. My dad thinks it's so adorable that everyone in our family has a yellow slicker. The Duck Family, he calls us. I think they're stupid.

"*Lissa*..." Mom said through clenched teeth.

"Okay, okay. Slickers." Boy, Jason sure could make things complicated. I was sure she'd never have thought of slickers if I were going alone.

"Jason, hurry up."

"I *am* hurrying, Lissa."

"Then hurry faster," I said. "At this rate the game will be over before we get there." Jason's idea of hurrying is anything that isn't actually standing still.

When we rounded the corner onto Laurel Street I let Jason trail behind while I made a detour to the juniper hedge in front of the Branson house. I slipped out of my raincoat, rolled it up in a ball and stuffed it in the hedge. That's what I usually do if I get stuck wearing it to school, unless it's actually pouring. Then, on the way home, I stop and retrieve it. It's a nearly perfect plan, except that my slicker always has a slightly putrid juniper-bush smell. But so far Mom hasn't noticed.

"Lissa, why did you put your raincoat in the bush?" Jason asked, coming up behind me.

"Never mind, Jason. Just hurry up."

"But *why*, Lissa?"

"Because it'll be safer there, Jason. Now hurry up."

"Let's make my coat safer, too."

"No, your coat's safer on you," I said.

"But *why*, Lissa?"

"Because, Squirt, it might rain on you. Now *hurry*."
Sometimes all Jason needs is an answer. He doesn't always bother to consider whether it makes sense.

We ended up late for the game anyhow, but it didn't seem to matter. I guess the only people who go to the games regularly are the parents of the players. So even with a few classmates and passersby thrown in, there was plenty of room in the bleachers to get a good seat. Jason and I parked ourselves in the middle section where we'd have a good view of everything. Not that Jason stayed there long. In about five minutes he was off, climbing to the top of the bleachers and then down to the bottom again and back, over and over.

Katie spotted me right away and waved. All the cheerleaders were wearing white shirts, white socks and their identical green skirts. I was impressed, they looked so official. Debra had a big green "C" sewn on the front of her shirt, and I spent a long time trying to figure out what it stood for. It wasn't for *Grasshoppers*, unless someone had made a mistake cutting it out. Maybe it meant *coordinated*. Or *cute*. Then it dawned on me that it probably meant *Captain*, since that's what they call the head of a cheerleading squad.

They had only learned four cheers well enough to do them for the game, and they just kept yelling the same four cheers over and over again. I was afraid the spectators would think it was a bit monotonous, but the cheers were so enthusiastic and so well synchronized that no one seemed to mind. In fact, after a while some of the people in the stands started yelling the cheers along with them.

33

At half time I asked Katie what the *C* on Debra's shirt stood for.

"Cheerleader," she said.

"That's *all?*" Good grief. How obvious. "I didn't think of that," I said. "But maybe you could suggest to Debra that it can stand for *Captain* instead. That might make more sense."

"Good idea," Katie said. "I'll mention it. Hey, we're all supposed to make green-and-white pom-poms before the next game. Do you want to help?"

"Sure," I said. Actually, I wasn't sure. I suddenly felt completely left out and fed up with the whole subject of cheerleaders. Making pom-poms was about the last thing I wanted to do. I wished I had stayed home.

The soccer team must have been short on enthusiasm, too. Or short on skill. But at any rate, the cheering didn't seem to be helping them much. By early in the second half they were behind 5–0. Plus it started to drizzle, and a lot of the neighborhood kids who had been hanging around left. I was tempted to leave, too, but I didn't know how Katie would take it.

I stared out over the field and tried to think of something to take my mind off feeling left out and miserable, and off the rain that was starting to trickle down the back of my neck. I began watching Joel—he was easy to keep track of with his red hair bobbing this way and that—and decided to count the number of times he hit the ball. Not too often, it turned out. I should have kept track of the times he fell down. The rain was making the field slick, and people were falling all over the place.

Still, Joel managed to kick the ball a few times, and even hit it with his knees a couple of times. That's one thing I'm sure I could never do, knee a ball. I have enough trouble connecting with my foot. I wondered if it was an advantage in soccer to have knobby knees. Did it make it easier to hit the ball? Or maybe that's how you *get* knobby knees. I'd never thought of that. Maybe I should ask Joel if he was sure this sport was good for him.

Thinking about asking Joel about his knees struck me as funny, and I began to cheer up.

Someone near me in the stands started to chuckle. Then several someones were chuckling. I thought for a minute that other people were thinking about Joel's knees, too. Then I heard a parent behind me say, "Oh, Charles, look at that little kid doing cheers. Isn't that just killing?"

I jerked my head around to look. Ohmigod, Jason.

"*Jason*," I screeched. I couldn't believe it. Jason was standing right at the end of the line of cheerleaders, his eyes glued on Debra, and a big, dopey grin on his face. He was doing a perfect imitation of the cheer they were doing, except he was doing it Jason-style, about two steps behind everyone else. Whenever someone stepped forward or to the left, Jason managed to step back or to the right, and he was thrusting his arms randomly, in all directions. Plus he was yelling at the top of his lungs. I never knew his voice could be so loud. He was yelling in his Jason-voice, all the words mispronounced.

Debra was carrying on with the cheer, but she kept giving him really dirty looks. And Sherry got out of line to try to push him out of the way. Jason was oblivious.

"*JASON!*" I screamed. "*JASON, COME HERE!*"

He either didn't hear or didn't care. I scrambled down the bleachers as fast as I could.

By now everyone had spotted him. The chuckles in the stands had turned to hoots and laughter. I tripped and banged my shin on the last bleacher, and as I stood up I saw the cheerleading squad execute the quick series of cartwheels and a leap that ended the cheer. Jason was right behind them. He started his "hero cartwheel" just as they started their final leap, and collided with Debra as she came down. They ended up in a heap, Jason whomped on his back, and Debra flung across him, face down in the mud.

"Ohmigod. Jason, are you okay?" I asked.

Jason grinned.

"Then get up!" I yelled. "You're not supposed to be here. Who told you you could do cheers, anyway?"

"You brat," Debra snarled at Jason as she stood up. "Get out of here."

"Come on, Jason," I said.

Debra was frantically trying to scrape mud off her face and clothes, without much success.

"You did this on purpose, Lissa," she said, turning on me. "You put your snotty little brother up to spoiling things just because I didn't choose you for cheerleader."

"I'm sorry," I said. "I mean, I *didn't,* but I'm sorry. Come on, Jason, let's get out of here." I grabbed Jason by the hand and tried to haul him away. But Jason was transfixed. He just stared open-mouthed at Debra, unable to move.

"Get him *out* of here!" Debra was beginning to yell. "Get him out, and get yourself out. Take your little retard-brother and leave!"

"He's not retarded," I said, hauling on Jason.

"He is, too," Debra said. "Everyone knows it. He can't even talk. Just listen to him."

"He's *not* retarded," I said hotly. "He's just a little kid." I was dimly aware that a crowd had begun to gather, but I wasn't embarrassed anymore. Debra was making me mad.

"If he's not a retard, then why can't he understand English?" she said, turning toward him. "I told you to *leave,* retard." She shoved him with a muddy hand.

"Keep your hands off him," I yelled. I felt my face get hot. I wanted to punch Debra. "There's nothing wrong with Jason, which is more than I can say for *some* people.

And I'm *glad* you fell in the mud. I didn't plan it, but I'm glad."

"You'll be sorry for this..." she hissed at me.

"Mud suits you, Debra. It really and truly does!" I grabbed Jason up in my arms and strode away.

It wasn't until we got to the edge of the park that I put him down. Then I held tight to his hand as we marched toward home. Jason was too dumbfounded to dawdle or protest. He just kept staring at me with his mouth open, as his short legs raced to keep up with mine.

"Lissa, you're wet," he said, finally.

"Just keep walking, Squirt. I'm not very happy with you, you know."

Jason sighed. "I know, Lissa. I know."

Mom and Dad came home from the gallery all bright-eyed and happy. The gallery was in the "perfect" location, the lighting was "marvelous" and the rental for the space was "very reasonable." They were definitely going to take it, and Dad started talking right away about which canvases he was going to have framed.

"Did you see some of the other artists' paintings?" I asked.

"Oh, yes," Mom said. "Most of the spaces are already rented and have things displayed."

"So how are they?" I asked. "Are any of them any good?"

"Definitely," Dad said. "I think there's a lot of first-rate talent represented there, Lissa. You'll have to come see it soon. Some of the paintings are superb."

That's what I was afraid of, that some of the other stuff might be good. I had this awful feeling that if Dad hung his paintings up in a real art gallery, they'd look pretty sad by comparison. He could be headed for a real disappointment.

Mom and Dad babbled on and on for the next forty-five

minutes about the gallery space, making plans and congratulating each other. They didn't bother to ask me a thing about the soccer game.

"Well, I'm glad *some*body had a good time today," I said at last.

"Oh, Lissa," Mom said, "I forgot about the game. Did your team win? Did Jason have a good time?"

"I wouldn't *know* if my team won because we had to leave early. And yes, Jason had a terrific time. That's why we left."

"I was a cheerleader," Jason said helpfully.

"Some cheerleader," I said. I told them how Jason made a spectacle of himself and tripped Debra, and how I ended up in an argument with her. But Dad seemed to think it was funny; his grin was getting wider by the minute. And Mom was tsk-tsking, only somehow it sounded insincere.

"I hope you realize it's not funny," I said. "Debra Dobbins probably hates me now, thanks to Jason."

"Debra's scary," Jason interjected. "She's more scary than a cricket. She's even as scary as an ant!"

Dad couldn't contain himself anymore and burst out laughing. It's not as if he hadn't heard Jason say that before, either. Jason's terrified of certain bugs, and whenever something scares him, he compares it to some insect. He has these Jason-logic explanations for it all. Crickets, for instance, he thinks are as big as dachshunds. He's only seen them in pictures, but he says he can tell their size from how loud they chirp. And he worries about ants because of how many of them arrive all at one time. He'll say, "What if they start to *grow?*"

"You should tell Debra that," Dad said between snorts and chortles. "Tell her your brother says she's as scary as an ant. *That'll* make her feel important."

Terrific, I thought. That's a big help. "Tell her yourself," I said. "Let me know how it works out."

5

KATIE PHONED me the next day and told me that Mr. Gonzales, the soccer coach, got mad, and now the cheerleaders were barred from the games. Evidently, when Debra fell down and we had our argument, some of the boys on the team had noticed. One of them even wandered off the playing field to see what was going on. And then Rob Ganz, who was playing goal, was watching us when the other team kicked the ball right past him and scored. He never even saw it.

Mr. Gonzales had a fit and said that the league rules "didn't provide for cheerleaders," that they were a distraction anyway, and that all the cheering in the world wasn't worth anything unless the team worked harder at practice, and so on and so forth. So, no cheerleaders allowed.

Katie said Debra was furious, mainly at me. She told everyone how it was all my fault, and described at great length how her mother had worked and slaved to make the skirts for everyone, and how upset she would be that it was all a waste. Debra kept saying that I had put my brother up to wrecking things because I was jealous that I wasn't chosen as a cheerleader. She even said that it was my fault the Grasshoppers lost, because when Rob missed the goal the team "got discouraged."

A lot of people agreed with Debra, Katie said, and were pretty mad at me, too. I wondered how many "a lot" was. At least Katie wasn't mad. She said it didn't matter all that much to her because she's so busy with gymnastics anyhow, and cheerleading was starting to look like it would take lots of time. And Rob wasn't mad either, she said, because he thought it was his own fault he didn't pay attention, and besides, they wouldn't have won in any case. At least there were some people left who didn't hold me responsible for everything. A few. Two, anyway.

Still, I was a nervous wreck walking to school on Monday. I tried walking very slowly. Then I tried walking backward, but that wasn't much help either. I figured that unless I actually went back home, I was still bound to get there eventually. It felt like I was walking to my own execution.

As soon as Katie saw me she said, "You don't look so good."

"I don't *feel* too good. Do you think I could be getting the flu?" I asked hopefully.

Katie put her hand on my forehead. "No ... you don't feel feverish or anything."

I braced myself and went into the coatroom to drop my stuff. Debra was in there already, and a crowd of girls was gathered around her, talking. They spotted me right away, and it suddenly got very quiet.

"Oh, gross," Sherry said in my direction.

"Here she comes—the spoiler," Tina chimed in.

I dropped my backpack on the floor and started to shrug off my jacket. "You can't blame me," I said. "It's not my fault the cheerleaders got disbanded."

"Oh, not much," Cindy said. "You put your dimwit little brother up to it, that's all. You got the whole cheerleading squad kicked out just because *you* were jealous."

"Yeah, and the Grasshoppers lost just because of you," someone else added.

"That's *ridiculous!*" I said. "A miracle couldn't have kept them from losing!"

Then I heard Bernice's whiny voice. "Yes, and Debra's mother did all that work. And those skirts were so-o-o beautiful. And now she's *heartbroken*."

I groaned.

"That's right," Tina said. "How would you like it if *your* mother spent all that time and money and worked so hard, and then someone ruined things so it's all a waste?"

"Look," I said, "it's not my fault Debra's mother spoils her rotten. *I* didn't tell her to make those stupid skirts, anyway. Debra did. So why don't you blame her!"

Debra was standing there with her arms folded, not saying a word. She didn't look grief-stricken about the skirts. She just looked smug. Almost pleased, I thought. Being an executioner must be pleasant work.

"We shouldn't bother to talk to Lissa," she said at last. "I mean you can't expect her to *care* that she ruined every-thing, since she did it on purpose and all. So *I* don't think we should spend any more time on her. In fact, I think it would be much nicer if we just didn't talk to her at all anymore. Don't you agree?"

41

"Oh, yeah. Right," Sherry said, and everyone else quickly murmured agreement. Off with my head . . . lop.

"Perfect," I said, pushing my way out of the coatroom. "That's just fine with me."

During Morning Meeting Katie and I sat together as usual. But it was funny, there was all this space around us. The rest of the girls were all sitting so tightly around Debra you'd have thought she'd smother. And everyone seemed to be making a special effort to be nice to her, as though there had been a death in her family or something.

When it was time to work, Mr. Shipley said that anyone who hadn't decided what they were doing for their spring social-studies project should look through a stack of books and magazines he'd brought, to see if they could get some ideas. And the people who had thought of something could go to the library to do research. I still hadn't thought of anything to do my project on, so I stayed in the room. I thought I'd be the only one, but nearly half the class stayed, too.

I'm not sure what Mr. Shipley expected, but I didn't think the books and magazines he had selected were exactly inspiring. Mostly they were about how some towns have town meetings, and others have a town council or a board of selectmen and things. It seemed like the kind of stuff you might have to memorize for a test, but you wouldn't want to do a whole report about it. Then I spotted a book called *Portrait of a Small Town*. It had lots of photographs and looked pretty interesting, so I reached for that one. Tina was standing right there, and as soon as I put my hand out, she snatched the book.

"I'm using this," she said.

Somehow I doubted that, but I said, "Let me have it after you, then."

"Cindy's using it next, *aren't* you, Cindy." She jabbed

Cindy with her elbow. Cindy looked confused for a second, then said, "Yeah, sure," and grinned. I got the message.

For the rest of the morning I sat at my desk trying to dream up a subject for my project, without much luck. I thought that if Tina put that book back on the table I'd make a dash for it and grab it. But she kept it at her desk. She never even opened it.

I had an idea that being not-very-popular was going to seem wonderful compared to having most of the class hate me. On a piece of binder paper I started a list headed "Friends." I wrote down Katie's name. Then I got stuck. I couldn't think of a single other girl. For boys, I put down Joel. Then I added an asterisk, and at the bottom of the page I wrote, "*Mostly in the summer."

"Don't let it upset you," Katie said at lunch time. "They'll get over it."

"Yeah, but will I care by the time I'm ninety-six years old?"

"It won't take till then."

"You want to bet? Debra strikes me as the kind with a long memory."

"She's just mad. But people don't stay mad forever, Lissa."

"You mean *you* don't," I said. That was just like Katie. She hardly ever *gets* mad, so of course she can't imagine anyone staying mad. But I could. I could imagine it quite well.

"Maybe I'll drop out of school," I said. "Did anyone ever drop out of school in the fifth grade? I may have to, anyway—I still haven't thought of anything to do for my social-studies report, and Mr. Shipley's going to kill me."

"You'll think of something soon," Katie said. "Here, have my candy bar. I think you need it more than I do."

Things are pretty bad when even chocolate doesn't taste

good. I ate it slowly, hoping that somewhere between the beginning and the end it would start to be delicious.

I was still working on it when Zack Brady came and plunked himself down on the bench between Katie and me.

"Do you two want some company?" he asked.

"Not much," I said. I wasn't sure I was in the mood for Zack right now.

"I mean," he went on, ignoring me, "I would have been here sooner, but it took a long time to beat my way through Lissa's crowd of admirers."

"Thanks a lot."

"Zack, if you came all the way over here to be sarcastic, maybe you should just leave," Katie said.

"No offense," he said. "Just a little levity. Thought it would brighten your day. Now that you're a member of the society, that is."

I could tell that Zack was working himself up to something he thought was highly amusing. His nostrils were flaring the way they do when he thinks something's hilarious but doesn't want to laugh.

I sighed. "Okay, Zack, what is it? What society? I give up."

"The Verruca Society, of course."

"So what's a verruca society?"

"It's an organization for all the people who have verrucae. Like *you*," he said, looking at me. He started to chuckle.

"Okay, Zack," I said. "You are now driving me crazy. Of course you don't *have* to tell me what verruca means. I can go look it up. Or I can ask someone else. Someone who's smarter than you. There *are* still some people left who are smarter than you, you know."

"Oh, it's no trouble," he said. "*Verruca* is the Latin word for 'wart.' Ugly, lumpy warts. And warts are contagious,

44

you know, because they're caused by a virus. So naturally nobody wants to be around people with warts. That's why I formed the Verruca Society—so all the warty people can have warty friends to associate with."

"Very funny, Zack. I don't happen to *have* warts, in case you hadn't noticed."

"Could have fooled me," he said. "And I'm an expert on warts, you know. I've had them myself for years. Trust me, Lissa—as of today you're covered with them."

"I'm not," I said. "And you don't have any warts, either, Zack. You don't even have any *freckles*. So quit pretending."

"Oh, but I *do* have warts. Thousands and thousands. It's a strange thing, though—sometimes the only people who can't see them are other people with warts." He wiggled his fingers at us like he was going to touch us.

"Cut it out," I said.

"That's not very nice," Katie said. "You're just making Lissa feel worse."

"Just trying to be helpful," he said, getting up. "After all, we warty people have to stick together. But now that you're a member of the society, I can let you in on a secret. That is, if you promise not to tell anyone."

"Am I supposed to plug my ears or what?" Katie asked. "I mean, if I don't have warts, am I allowed to hear?"

"Oh, it's okay to listen," he said, his nostrils twitching again. "I told you—verrucae are contagious. You'll probably have them yourself pretty soon."

Katie groaned.

"Just go away, Zack," I said.

"Oh, I will. But first the society secret," he said, looking around as if to check that no one else was listening. Which was dumb because there wasn't anyone within miles. "Debbie Dobbins is really an airhead," he whispered loudly. "And she's not even cute, she's just short."

"Nobody else thinks that," Katie said.

"Well, I'd tell them, but you see nobody ever listens to people with warts. They don't want to get that close." He wiggled his fingers at us again and went off, laughing maniacally.

I was about to laugh, too, but Katie didn't look especially amused, so I stifled it.

"The thing about Zack," Katie said as we went to dump our things in the garbage, "is that he doesn't really seem to care that nobody likes him. I mean, if he would just try a little harder to blend in, he might have some friends."

"Oh, I don't know," I said. "I don't really mind him all that much. I mean, I know he's obnoxious and all, but I guess I'm just used to him the way he is."

The afternoon was a little better than the morning because we had math, which I always love. There's something I find relaxing about sitting there working out problems. Katie thinks that's the oddest thing she's ever heard. She says I'm the only person she knows who gets relaxed doing percentages.

During math, Zack kept pelting me with little bits of paper. At first I was annoyed because I didn't know who was doing it. I thought someone was trying to harass me. But then I opened up one of the papers, and it said, "Wart People Unite!" so I knew right away. Almost every time Mr. Shipley turned his back, one hit me. They said things like "Watch who you touch!" and "Compound W won't help!" and "Wart Power!" I turned to look at Zack, who quickly clasped his hands on his desk and looked at the ceiling with a not-quite-angelic smirk. He really knows how to milk a joke.

When I got one that said, "Guard the Society Secret!" I started to laugh. I clapped my hand over my mouth and the laugh came out my nose instead.

"Lissa and Zack," Mr. Shipley said. "Would you be interested in staying after school to discuss appropriate classroom behavior with me?"

"Not really," I said, turning beet red.

"Sorry, sir. I have other plans," Zack said.

"Then if you don't want to *change* your plans..." Mr. Shipley said, glaring at Zack.

"Ohhhh...Lissa and Zack," came a voice from the other side of the room. It was Debra, and right away about three other people said "Oh, ohhh..." and "Whoa..."

Just what I needed. Now everyone was going to think I liked Zack. I made sure all my books were organized in a stack before the final bell rang and was the first one out of the class.

6

I DRAGGED a chair into the front hall and taped a note to it, so Mom couldn't miss it when she came in.

To Whom It May Concern:
   If certain people would leave work on *time*, certain other people wouldn't have to sit around by themselves waiting for someone to get home. In case anyone cares!

                           Love XXOO,
                           Melissa Woodbury
P.S. I went to the park. I'll be back soon.
P.S. Again. Say Hi to Jason.

I know I'm not supposed to mind it, since I'm nearly eleven years old and all, but I hate it when I'm the first one home. The house seems so lonely or something. Sometimes, if Mom knows she has to go somewhere after work, she lets me pick Jason up at the sitter's. Which I really like, because Jason always acts overjoyed to see me. And he's not even pokey on the way home. Then if I'm in an extra good mood I read him a story, which he loves. He squishes up real close to me and I can feel him breathing. It's funny . . . at all the exciting parts he holds his breath.

I wasn't exactly going to the park. I was going to the creek, which is right next to the park. Same thing, I thought. I parked my bike against the chain-link fence. There were two granola bars in my basket, which I had raided from the kitchen to bring along. I stuffed them in my pockets and climbed through the fence.

"Hey, Lissa!"

I turned around. "Joel! Hi!"

"What are you doing here?"

"I could ask you the same thing," I said.

"Oh. Well, I've been coming here after school most days. I'm checking the water. See, it suddenly dawned on me that we spent all that time last summer digging when the creek was dry and the banks were hard. I thought I could do some digging when the banks were still wet."

"Yeah, but that's dangerous, Joel. I mean you could drown." I could see it now. Everyone would blame me for that, too.

"No . . . but that's why I'm checking the water. I'm waiting until it gets low enough."

"Oh, well, that's okay, then."

"It's less than a foot deep now," he said. "I was going to do some excavating today. Want to help?"

"Sure," I said. I was starting to cheer up. "Hey, Joel, you know what?"

49

"What?"

"I'm really glad we know about the Indians. Only its kind of sad that nobody else does. I mean, in the whole town of Westmont you'd think someone would act interested."

"Yeah, I know," Joel said.

"I mean, they don't even know what's been happening right in their own *town*," I repeated.

That's when I got my bright idea. It was almost like a light bulb flashed on, just like in the comics.

"Hey, Joel! What are you doing for your social-studies project? Did you think of anything?"

"Yeah, I was thinking of doing a report on the Westmont Fire Department. My uncle's a fireman, you know, and he talks about it all the time..."

"Well, I just had this great idea. Why not do a project about the Ohlone Indians? That's part of our town. Or at least it's a part of our history, so that makes it just as important, doesn't it? And it would be original—I'm sure no one else has thought of it."

"Hey, yeah, that's a good idea. And you can tell about the clams and oysters, because that's about our resources in a way. Mr. Shipley will probably like it a lot."

"Yeah, well, what I thought is...We could do it together. If you want to, that is. We're allowed to work in pairs, and the Indians sort of belong to both of us, if you know what I mean."

"Yeah, I do," he said. "Okay, let's. That would be fun. And if we do more excavating before then, we might even find a bone or something to take in."

I felt both excited and relieved. At least I wouldn't have to drop out of school for flunking social studies. "Here, Joel. I was going to eat both of these, but you can have one," I said, handing him a granola bar.

"You know, Joel, I'm really glad you're not mad at me. Everyone else is."

"Not everyone," he said. "Anyhow, it's not your fault we lost that game. The Trojans are the best team in the league. No way we were going to beat them."

"Tell that to Debra Dobbins," I said. "It might help her to figure things out."

"She's just upset because the cheerleaders were kicked out of the game. You can't blame her for that. Anyhow," he added, "I think she can figure things out without my help."

"I wouldn't be too sure about that, Joel. She's saying a lot of nasty things about me. Besides, Zack Brady says she's an airhead."

"Say, what is it with you and Zack, anyway? Do you really like him or something?"

"Don't be a jerk—of course not. But he's right about some things."

"Well, I think Debra's nice," he said.

"Ick."

"Well, I do. Plus she has a good personality."

"*Joel*. You can't really think that. Debra Dobbins has a personality like a vampire!"

"Come on, Lissa . . . She does not."

"She does. There's not a single nice thing about Debra, Joel. She's not even really cute. People just think she is."

Joel stared at the ground for a second without saying anything. But then when he spoke it was in this very soft voice. "Well, I think she's pretty. She has really beautiful hair . . ."

"*Joel Osborne* . . ."

He liked her. I mean *like* liked her. I couldn't believe it. How stupid. I should have figured. I think I just stood there with my mouth open for a minute.

51

"I have to go," I said. "It's getting late. I have to go home."

"Lissa, you just got here..."

"You're so dumb, Joel Osborne. I never knew you could be so dumb."

"Lissa, what..."

"And you can just do your dumb fire-department project by yourself, Joel. I wouldn't work on any project with someone so dumb."

"But, *Lissa*..." he called after me.

"Just *shut up*, Joel."

I put my bike in the garage and stomped up the back steps. Slowly and loudly. Mom's car was in the driveway, and I figured she might as well know a mad person was coming in.

She was at the kitchen sink doing dishes. And humming. "Oh, Lissa, there you are," she said in this very cheerful voice. "I'm glad you're home. Jason has a surprise for you."

"I was home earlier," I said pointedly, "only nobody else was."

"Yes, I know, dear. I got your note."

"And I sat around here for a whole half-hour waiting for someone to show up."

"Lissa, dear..."

"But that's okay. Don't feel you have to apologize or anything."

"Lissa...."

"I'm sure nobody would care if I spent the rest of my life alone."

"Lissa, I don't know what's bothering you, but if you'd just..."

"I wonder how *you'd* like it, though, if nobody cared..."

"Melissa Woodbury, stop it!"

I stopped.

"Now. If you would just *think* you'd realize that today is Monday, and Jason has speech therapy on Mondays."

"Oh." Oops.

"Now, is something bothering you?"

"I guess not." All at once I was feeling very wrung out.

"Good. Now would you like to know what Jason's surprise is?"

"I guess so."

"Jason," Mom called. "Lissa's home. Would you like to come say hello?"

Jason came and stood in front of me with his big, dopey grin on his face. He just stood there and stared.

I looked at Mom. This was getting boring.

"You might try saying hello to him first, Lissa."

"Hi, Jason," I said.

"Hi, Lissa." He said it very carefully.

It took a second to sink in. Then I realized what he had done.

"Jason, you learned my name! Do that again," I said, grabbing him.

"Hi, Lissa," he said, laughing.

"That's *perfect.* You can really do it. You didn't say 'Witha,' and you didn't say 'Wissa.'"

"I can do it again," he said. "Do you want me to do it again?"

"Yes!"

"Lissa!"

"Oh, Jason, you're the best. You're really super."

"I know, Lissa. Now stop kissing me. I hate kisses."

That night I took out my list of friends. I crossed out Joel's name. Then I wrote down Zack. Then I thought a while. Then I wrote down JASON WOODBURY.

53

7

I WAS REALLY GLAD when Friday came. Not just because I was going to spend the night at Katie's, which I was, but also because the rest of the week hadn't been much better than Monday.

First of all, I made up my mind on Tuesday just to act like everything was normal. Mom used to say if someone is being mean to you, the best thing to do is just ignore it. Then they get bored and stop. So I decided that was the best approach—to act as if I didn't care.

Lunch times were easy, since I always eat with Katie, anyhow. I just made it a point not to look over to where Debra was sitting with her cronies, in case they were giving me dirty looks or anything.

In class it was a little harder, what with being all stuffed in the same room and everything. About the only thing I could think of that would show everyone how unconcerned I was would be to go stand in the front of the room, smile blissfully at everyone, then go sit back down. That would have gotten the message across, but I thought it would be slightly obvious.

So I decided I'd simply act fascinated by my schoolwork. Mr. Shipley wasn't much help in that department because he started right out on Tuesday by giving us a real stupid composition to write. It was supposed to be about spring, and what we liked about it. I hate that kind of thing. I just can't get all excited about nature on cue. But I sat there, trying to look absorbed, and ended up writing this very enthusiastic essay about how I like spring because then the rainy season ends and you don't have to worry about stepping on a disgusting snail every time you walk out the door. I'm pretty sure it wasn't what Mr. Shipley had in mind, but there wasn't enough time to start over.

Anyhow, I guess ignoring people who are being mean to you only works with little kids. Or maybe Debra doesn't get bored all that easily. Because on Wednesday there was a sign taped to the mirror in the girls' room that said, "ATTENTION! IMPORTANT NOTICE! READ CAREFULLY! Everyone who likes Lissa Woodbury sign below!"

There was only one signature: Bernice's. And she had crossed it out. Typical. I mean someone probably had to explain it to her... "No, Bernice, the idea is to *not* sign it."

Debra had put the notice up, of course. I could tell right away because Debra always dots her *i*'s with little circles. I suppose she thinks it's adorable.

What really made me mad, though, was that she had done it in color. Four colors. She had used my four-color pen.

Thursday morning, right when everyone was gathering

55

for Morning Meeting, I marched up to Debra and demanded my pen back.

"I don't have any pen of yours," she said.

"You do, too. I loaned you my four-color pen a long time ago, and you never gave it back."

"I told you, Lissa. I don't have any smelly pen of yours. So quit bothering me."

"You *do*," I insisted. "You used it. You used it on that note you hung up in the girls' room. So you can just give it back."

"Oh, *that* pen. Well, sorry, Lissa, but that's *my* pen. Lots of people have them, you know. You aren't the only one." She said it in this nasty-sweet kind of voice, very superior sounding.

"Liar!" I practically screamed. She was making me so mad. "Give it back!"

Just then Mr. Shipley walked in. He must have heard me because he cleared his throat and said, "Some problem, Lissa?"

That embarrassed me, and without thinking I answered, "Yes, Debra has something of mine and she won't give it back." As soon as I said it, I wished I hadn't. Nobody likes it if you whine to a teacher about some argument with another kid.

"It's just not true, Mr. Shipley," Debra said in this very reasonable tone. "Lissa thinks just because I have a pen like hers that I stole it. But lots of people have those pens. You shoudn't accuse someone of stealing unless you can prove it, should you, Mr. Shipley? Can't you get sued for that?"

"Well . . . ahem . . . it's certainly not very nice to . . . ahem . . . make a public accusation of that nature unless you can back it up," he said. He was looking at me, and managing to sound very stuffy and formal. "Perhaps you ladies could meet with me after school to see if we can straighten this out."

"Oh, but that's not *fair*," Debra squealed. "I'm supposed to go right after school to get my hair cut."

"Lissa?"

"Oh, forget it," I said. "It's not worth it." It wasn't, either. I couldn't actually *prove* it was my pen, and besides, everybody would just think I was a crybaby. I sat down feeling mad and helpless. There didn't seem to be any way to win with Debra.

"I didn't notice that Debra's hair looked any shorter today, did you?" I asked Katie. We were trudging up Sierra Drive after school on Friday, on our way to Katie's house.

"Oh," Katie said. She looked startled. "I didn't really pay any attention. But come to think of it, I don't think it did. Good grief."

"That's okay," I said. "I don't think Mr. Shipley noticed, either."

We walked on in silence for a few more minutes. Then I realized I didn't want to think about Debra anymore. It put me in a crummy mood, and I was sick of it.

"I'm really glad you asked me over," I said, shifting my backpack on my back. It was stuffed full with my overnight things and some *Mad* magazines in case we got bored.

"Me, too," she said. "And my mother. She really likes you."

"I know. I like her, too."

That's one of the best things about going to Katie's house. She has the world's nicest mother. Mrs. Hutchinson always gives me a big hug when she sees me, not like most people's mothers who just say, "Hi." I don't know whether she especially likes me, or if it's only because I'm Katie's friend. But it always makes me feel good.

And I like Katie's house. Or condominium. It's like a two-story apartment that's attached to other two-story apartments, and I can never figure out if it's more like an apartment or a house. But Katie says it's actually a condominium.

Katie and her mother live there alone because Katie's father died when she was little. She doesn't really remember him very well, she says, so she doesn't feel too sad about it or anything. There's a picture of him in the living room, and he has a nice face with a nose just like Katie's. Katie says she thinks her mother will get remarried some day, and I get the impression that Katie wishes it would be sooner rather than later. She says she thinks her mother is being too picky. But mostly they seem perfectly happy just the way they are.

As soon as we walked in, Mrs. Hutchinson gave Katie a big hug and kiss, and then she gave me a hug.

"Lissa, it's so good to see you. How are your parents? How's Jason?"

"Oh, they're fine, thanks. Jason's fine. He learned to say my name right, and he's been doing it all week. It's really neat. He's not really dumb, you know. He just has this speech problem." I don't know what made me say that. It just popped out.

"I never thought he *was* dumb, Lissa. You know, I have a forty-year-old sister who lisps, and she's a research chemist. I wouldn't call that dumb, would you?"

"No," I said. "I sure wouldn't. Of course, Jason has more than a lisp. It's like his tongue totally malfunctions on most words. But he's improving really fast."

"I knew he would," she said. "I'm very glad to hear that." That's the thing about Mrs. Hutchinson. She always makes everyone feel good about everything.

Mrs. Hutchinson made us tacos for dinner, which is one of my favorites. My mom hardly ever makes them because it makes such a mess in the kitchen. Katie and I helped with grating the cheese and chopping up the lettuce and tomatoes. Then for dessert we had raspberry-cheesecake ice cream from Lyle's Ice Cream. After dinner we went up to Katie's room and got out the board games. We played Parcheesi once. We each took two colors, and Katie came in first and fourth; I came in second and third. Then we played three games of Clue, which I love, even though Katie beat me twice.

Katie has the most beautiful room. It has powder blue wall-to-wall carpet, and curtains with little blue- and rose-colored flowers on them, which happen to match her bedspread. But the best thing is, she has a canopy bed. If I had a canopy bed, I'd never get out of it. But for some weird reason Katie thinks it's fun to sleep on the floor. So we both spread our sleeping bags out there, side by side.

When we were in our pj's, we made popcorn and then watched an old horror movie on TV. We made fun of all the lame parts that were supposed to be scary but weren't, and got hysterical. We also got popcorn in our sleeping bags and had to shake them out before we could go to sleep.

"Spending the night here is the most fun I've had all week," I said after we had turned out the lights.

"Me, too," Katie said. "But other good things have happened this week, if you think about it."

"Like what?"

"Like Jason learning to say your name. Oh, and Mr. Shipley liked your project idea."

"That's true," I said. "That's three."

Katie giggled. "If you look at it the right way, three's really a lot."

"I suppose so," I said. "It's just that when you have sixteen lousy things happen in the same week, it tends to dilute it a little." I started giggling, too. Nothing seemed that bad anymore.

"Anyhow," Katie went on, "I still think Debra's going to forget all about being mad at you soon. Especially now that she has her new club to think about."

59

"*What club?* Katie, what are you talking about?"

"Didn't anyone *tell* you? Debra's organizing a club. Everyone was talking about it today."

"But nobody talks to me, remember?"

"Yeah, but I guess I thought you'd at least overhear," she said. "Well, anyway, it's supposed to be very exclusive. That's Debra's word, exclusive. You have to get an invitation to join. It's called FUNCHY, and everything else about it is a secret."

"Oh, come on, Katie. You *have* to tell me."

"No," she said, "I can't. That is, I don't know. Nobody knows unless they're a member."

That figured. I mean Debra would really adore the drama of a secret club.

"FUNCHY is kind of a bimbo-sounding name," I said. "It reminds me of a breakfast cereal. Jason would love it. He'd probably give up Kix. What's it mean, anyhow?"

"I don't know that either. I think it's supposed to be part of the secret."

"Oh, wonderful. Well, I wonder if anyone has bothered to mention to Debra that secret clubs are illegal in our school." Maybe they do things differently where Debra came from, but our school has always had a rule against secret clubs. In fact, almost any kind of club is out, unless it's Girl Scouts or something. It says so right in the little mimeographed handbook they give us every year. It's right next to the rule about no bare feet.

"I forgot about that," Katie said. "Maybe someone should tell her."

"Naw," I said, "I'd rather just let her get in trouble all by herself. As Debra would say, that would be more fair, don't you agree? Since it was *her* idea and all..."

I can always tell when Dad's painting because the whole house reeks of linseed oil and turpentine. To find him, all you have to do is follow the fumes. I dropped my sleeping bag in my room and went into the studio.

"It stinks in here," I said.

"Oh, hi! Did you have a good time at Katie's?"

"Naturally," I said, hugging him.

"You know, Lissa, you're supposed to love this smell. It should be in your blood by now. After all, you've lived with it all your life."

"I'm sure it *is* in my blood," I said. "It probably got in through my nose. But it still stinks."

Dad just laughed. "Here, come take a look at this," he said, waving a brush at the canvas he was working on. "What do you think?"

I really wish my father wouldn't ask me what I think of his paintings. They're always these abstract things, and I can never figure out what they're supposed to be about. My favorite paintings are the kind they have in the museum, where all the objects look so real you feel like you could just pluck them off the canvas.

"So what's it supposed to be?" I asked.

"You tell me. What does it make you think of?"

"Oh, Dad, please..." I said in my long-suffering tone of voice. "Maybe you could just give me a hint?"

"Come on, try," he said. "Just look at it a minute, Lissa. See what comes to mind."

I sighed and stared at the canvas. It was huge, well over a yard square, and up in the left-hand corner was a little area of blue, white and green. The rest of it was all in ugly browns, about six different shades of them. What came to mind was that he should start over.

"Mud," I finally pronounced. Might as well be honest.

"Great! That's exactly right," Dad enthused. "It's called *Spring*—you're developing quite an eye, my girl."

"Oh, no," I groaned. Just what I needed, to develop

61

"an eye" for this junk. "That doesn't even make sense. I mean, there aren't any birds or flowers or anything."

"But don't you see, your *instinct* was right," Dad said. "You got the sense of all that damp, spring earth. And up there in the corner are the first shoots of new foliage."

I give up. I absolutely give up. I only hoped he wouldn't hang it in his gallery space. It would drive everyone away.

"Dad," I said at last, "I've got this instinct that this room would look better as a bedroom. Don't you? I mean, think of it—a canopy bed right over there." I gestured to where his easel was standing. "And some pretty wallpaper. And maybe a carpet instead of this tarp. Lavender would be nice. Wall-to-wall..."

"Lissa, where would I paint?"

"The garage?" What a great idea. Why didn't I think of that years ago. "You could use the garage! We never park the car in there, anyhow, and the bikes don't take up all that much room."

"The garage is far too cold for me to paint in, Lissa. My hands would get numb; I wouldn't be able to paint at all."

Hmmm. Worse things could happen, I thought.

"Well, if I'm never going to have my own room, could I at least have a canopy bed?" If I had a canopy bed, one of the first things I'd do is hang blankets and sheets from the top, in case I felt like being alone. Then I'd be all enclosed. It would be the next best thing to a room of my own.

"You have a perfectly good bed right now, Lissa. We can't afford to go spending money on things we don't need. Now, of course, when I start selling some of my paintings..."

"That's okay," I said. I mean, I wasn't going to start holding my breath or anything. "I think I'll just go into my noisy, overcrowded room and do some homework."

As I left, Dad started squeezing some more brown onto his palette. Burnt umber. It looked really gross.

8

DEBRA HAS BEEN having a wonderful time. Since nobody can get into the FUNCHY Club without an invitation from her, people are knocking themselves out to be nice to her. It seems like every single girl wants to be in the club, and they're all nearly falling over each other trying to be especially helpful or generous or complimentary to her, or whatever else they think might work. If she drops a pencil on the floor, at least two people make a grab for it and then whoever gets it sharpens it first before handing it back to her.

I'd be surprised if she's had to do her math homework more than once in the last two and and a half weeks. Someone always makes an extra copy of their homework and gives it to her. Plus, you'd think that every item of clothing she wore was brand new. Debra usually does have a steady supply of new clothes, but even if she's wearing a sweater she's worn twenty times before, someone is sure to say, "Oh, Debra, you look so nice. That's a really beautiful sweater."

Mostly Debra just smiles sweetly and says, "Thank you." She doesn't hand out invitations for just any old thing. You have to really work at it.

In the two and a half weeks since she started it, she's given out seven invitations to join FUNCHY. Naturally, Sherry and Tina got theirs right away. But since then, Debra's been giving someone an invitation only once every two or three days. I don't know how many people she's planning to invite altogether, but she's sure making the most of it in the meantime.

Bernice is being really pitiful. She's just *sure* she's going to get her invitation any day now, and she follows Debra around everywhere like she's her shadow, making a big fuss over her. You'd think Debra would get sick of always having Bernice right behind her, but she doesn't seem to mind.

Personally I think Bernice is wasting her time. I mean, being wonderful to Debra has never gotten Bernice anywhere before, so I don't know why she thinks it's going to work this time.

Today, as everyone was coming in from lunch recess, Marla was all ecstatic because she had gotten an invitation to FUNCHY. She was babbling on about how she just couldn't figure out what to wear for her first day—tomorrow.

Bernice said, "Oh, wear something pretty. You just *have* to wear something pretty. Everyone does." I guess she thinks she's a big authority, since she's so obsessed with the club.

Tina gave Bernice this exasperated, who-do-you-think-you-are look, and explained very patiently, "You should wear something nice, Marla. But it doesn't have to be your best clothes. Just something nice for the ceremony."

"What ceremony?" Zack butted in. "What's the big deal ceremony? Does she have to go around and kiss everyone's feet, or do you just stick her with one of those cheap little pins?" All the girls in FUNCHY wear these little safety pins with green and yellow beads on them. I haven't figured out how they get the beads on the pins yet, but I'm working on it. One thing about Zack—he notices things.

"Mind your own business, Zack," Tina said.

"Anyway, it's *secret*," Bernice said.

"Well, anyone can see those stupid pins. So I wouldn't call that very secret. The only secret left, so far as I can tell, is what's so great about sitting around an old stump together at lunch time. Unless it's a club for worshipping old stumps. Maybe that's it."

"It's not," Bernice said hotly. "It's *much* more important than that."

"Yeah, it is," Tina said. Then she added, "Though of course Bernice doesn't know what it *is* about, since she's not a member herself..."

"Well, good luck," Zack said, clapping Bernice on the back. "I hope it lives up to all your expectations, Bernice. 'Cause I've examined that old stump, and just between you and me, it has *worms*."

"I hate you!" Bernice yelled, and burst into tears. I guess she didn't like being reminded that she's not in FUNCHY yet. Or else she just hates not knowing things. But Tina said, "You're such a creep, Zack. You don't know anything. You don't know what you're talking about."

"Oh dear," he replied, with a look of mock horror, "does this mean my invitation will be delayed? I *do* hope not. I was *so* counting on it." And he headed off to his seat in a fit of laughter.

The purpose of FUNCHY Club *is* a well-kept secret. I have to admit, even Katie and I have been getting curious. Not that I want to join or anything, but I guess that when there's a secret I naturally get very nosey and want to know all about it.

Katie thinks maybe it's some sort of self-improvement club because Debra has been acting nicer since she started it. But I think Debra is just enjoying having everyone follow her around all the time, which isn't the same as becoming a nice person.

Anyhow, as I pointed out to Katie, she's only nicer to Katie, not to me. It's true that she's not as nasty to me anymore, but I get the impression that it's just too much trouble right now. Whereas with Katie it's more like she's going out of her way to be thoughtful. For instance, she told Katie there was a show coming up on TV about kids who were future Olympic hopefuls, and that she should be sure to watch. And another time, Debra said she'd seen a package of stickers in a store that said "Property of Katie" on them and was thinking of buying them for her.

I'm not too crazy about the idea that Debra has decided to be wonderful to Katie. Maybe it's because it's so awkward at times, like when Debra walks up and starts talking to Katie while I'm standing there. Debra acts like I'm not even there, and I begin to feel all squirmy. I get the feeling that Debra despises me just as much as ever, but she's saving up until she can think of something really mean to do.

Katie says I've developed a suspicious mind where Debra is concerned, and I guess she's right.

9

"Jason, move. You're in my way," I said.

Jason moved back about a quarter of an inch.

"Farther than that, Jason. Come on."

He scooted back about another quarter of an inch.

"Jason . . . you're driving me crazy. I can't get anything done with you breathing on me and getting your head in the way."

"But I want to help, Lissa."

"You can't help. I told you a thousand times already, you can't help with this."

At the rate things were going, I was sure I'd never get my social-studies project done. There were still three weeks left to go before they were due, but I had the distinct

67

impression that most people were nearly finished already. I had barely started.

Joel came over last week to borrow some Scotch tape, and he said his report on the fire department was nearly done. Then he asked me how my project was going. I really could have used his help, and I almost asked him if he'd like to work with me after all. But I guess I was still too mad at him, so I just said, "Fine," and handed him the tape.

It wasn't going fine at all. First of all I had a hard time even thinking of something to do. I mean, I knew I was going to report about the Ohlone Indians, but I couldn't figure out how to do it except to bring in a bunch of the shells we collected and talk about them. The thing is, you have to have something interesting to show people when you give a report, or they all get bored and restless, or practically fall asleep.

I got this idea of doing a graph about the Ohlones, to show that they lived here for thousands of years, as compared to a crummy two hundred years for the white man. So I spent half a day counting little squares on graph paper, then taping the paper together. Jason kept trying to help me count but he can only count to thirty. He goes, "twenty-seven, twenty-eight, twenty-nine, thirty, a googol," because he thinks anything over thirty is so big that it has to be a googol. Naturally I got all mixed up in my counting and had to start over twice. The trouble was, when I finally got it done it was a stupid looking graph. It was ten feet long and five inches wide.

Then I had this idea that I'd write a play about the Ohlones. I can almost see them in my mind when I think about them, and I thought that if other people could imagine what they were like, they'd care about them a lot, too. But for one thing nobody has ever given a play for a report before, so I was worried that maybe it wasn't allowed.

Then I realized I'd need quite a few people to put on a play. What a joke that would be. Instead of a cast of thousands, I'd be lucky to have a cast of three, including Jason. A play is definitely a project for someone who has lots of friends.

That's the way it went. For days, every time I tried to think of something, I thought blanks. Then I got my best idea when I had given up ever thinking of anything. Actually, I was working on a time-and-motion problem for my math homework when it popped into my head: I'd do a model of an Ohlone Indian village.

Dad got all excited about the project and found a thin piece of plywood for me to use as a base. I painted it all brown, except for a creek along one edge, which I made a kind of tannish blue. Then I squirted tons of Elmer's all over the brown part, and sprinkled lots of dirt from Mom's dead garden all over it. Enough of the dirt stuck to make it look like real earth.

The dome-shaped tule-grass huts stumped me for quite a while. If I'd done this project in September it would be okay, because there's nothing but dried grass everywhere in September. But in March, all the grass is wet and green, so I had to improvise. I ended up making the houses out of papier-mâché. Papier-mâché is incredibly messy, and I hate all the cleaning up you have to do when you make something from it. It takes ages. But the huts looked okay when I was done.

The fun part, though—the part Jason wanted to help with—was making the Indians. Mom dug out a bunch of clay that was stored in the garage. She bought it one time when she was on a pottery-making kick. She made pots for weeds, and other equally unpractical things. But she gave it up after a while, and the clay had been sitting in the garage ever since.

First I went to the library and checked out the only book

they have with a picture of an Ohlone Indian in it. It seemed important to me to make the Indians look like they really did look, maybe because I think it's so unfair that everyone has forgotten about them. The photograph in the book was of a woman, and I suppose it was taken pretty soon after cameras were invented—it wasn't too clear. Of course, by then the Ohlones were almost all living in missions, so the Indian in this picture was just wearing regular clothes.

But what I noticed about it, the first time I saw it, was how sad the woman looked. She just looked like an Indian woman dressed up in white people's clothes, with a terribly sad expression. I stared at it a long time, sitting at a table in the library, and pretty soon I began to feel sad, too. After a while—maybe it was because the fluorescent lamp overhead was flickering—it seemed to me that her lower lip was quivering, just as if she were about to cry.

I knew then that I didn't want to make my clay Indians look like just nobody. I wanted them to be real. That's why it was taking me so long to make them.

I had some that were sitting down with their legs under them, and some that were standing up. I tried to make them look sturdy. Not fat exactly, but a little plump. The Ohlones always had plenty to eat, so none of them were scrawny. Personally, I'd be thin as a skeleton if I had to eat the stuff they lived on. Not just shellfish and acorns, but deer and rabbits and grass seeds and things. They even ate gophers and grasshoppers. Yech. But I guess they liked it, because they were all well fed and happy.

That was the other thing. I wanted my Indians to be cheerful, round-faced and smiling, not sad like the woman in the photograph. Because they were happy people before they got put into missions, and that's the way they should have stayed.

"If I can't help, what *can* I do?" Jason asked.

70

"Watch," I said. "You can watch if you stay out of my way."

"Watching's no fun, Lissa."

"So go do something else." He was really exasperating me. "Leave and find something of your own to do. Just quit bugging me."

"I don't *want* to leave, Lissa. I want to watch. Why can't I watch?"

"*SO WATCH*," I shouted. "Good grief, Jason. You can really be impossible, you know that?"

"I know, Lissa," he said with a sigh.

I wish Jason wouldn't sigh when I get mad at him. It always makes me feel guilty, even when it's his own fault. But at least he watched quietly for a while, so I was able to make a little progress.

I was getting worried about whether I should make some Indian babies. There would have been babies in the village, but it was hard enough just to make the grown-ups. Working on something as small as babies would be impossible. I'd need a magnifying glass. Plus they'd have to be in baskets because that's how the Ohlones kept their babies. Finally I decided babies would just be too complicated, so if anybody asked I would say they were all having naps in the huts. That sounded reasonable enough.

"How many Indians are you going to make, Lissa? A googol?"

"No, Jason. Maybe around thirteen," I said. "I have other things to make, too, you know. Like a grass boat, and some baskets and lots of other things if I have time."

Thinking about all the things I still wanted to make was almost scary. If I did everything, and tried to make it realistic looking, I could spend the rest of the year on it. The Indians alone were taking me a whole afternoon each, and I only had five so far.

"Are you going to give them clothes?" Jason asked.

"Well, I'll give the ladies skirts, because they wore skirts. But the men didn't wear any clothes."

"But, Lissa, they have to wear clothes. I get goose bumbles without my clothes!"

"Goose *bumps*," I corrected. "Anyway, I guess the Indians didn't. Besides, when it was really cold the men wore fur capes sometimes. Or they covered their bodies with mud."

"But, Lissa, mud's *dirty*," he said, looking astonished.

"That depends," I said.

"Depends on what?"

"It just depends, Jason. Like probably you don't think mud's dirty if you're used to it. Like the Indians were."

"How did they get used to it?"

"Oh, Jason, don't ask me. It wasn't my idea. They just did, I guess."

"Oh," he said, with a perplexed expression, "I see." Then he was quiet for a while, and I scratched hair on the model I was making.

I thought it was handy that the Indians didn't wear many clothes, because I could just see myself trying to make tiny little clothes for all of them. I'd be grown up before I finished. On the other hand, I didn't particularly want to cause a sensation by taking naked Indians to school. That could be embarrassing. So when I told Mom I had this dilemma, she suggested that I just make the men "anatomically incorrect" and "be a bit vague about the women." She said that if it was good enough for the people who make dolls, it ought to be good enough for me. When she put it that way, it seemed sensible, so that's what I did.

"I'm going to be an Indian when I grow up, Lissa."

"You can't be an Indian, Jason."

"Yes I can," he said.

"No you can't, so just forget it. Only little Indians grow up to be Indians. And you're not, so forget it."

"I *can*," he said firmly. "You'll see I can." He practically glared at me, then he suddenly stood up and left the room.

Fine, I thought. Knowing Jason, his next move would be to go ask Dad if he could be an Indian. And Dad would say, "Sure," and then Jason would have another crack-brained idea to add to his collection. I was tempted to follow Jason out of the room just so I could give Dad a lecture. Then I thought that since Dad never listens to me, anyhow, I might as well stay put. At least Jason was out of my hair for a while. I was *sure* this project would go faster if I had a room of my own.

I got to work in peace for about an hour. I just kind of hummed along, enjoying the feel of the clay. The Indian I was working on seemed especially nice. I almost felt like I should give her a name.

Then the quiet was shattered by the sound of Mom having a hollering fit.

"What in the name of heaven did you *do?*" she yelled. "Since when do you behave like this? You're in big trouble, young man. You come with me right this minute!"

I had to run to see what was going on, naturally. I could tell she was yelling at Jason, and since my parents almost never yell at Jason I knew it had to be monumental.

I caught up with them in the back hall, headed outside. Jason was completely naked except for Mom's old mink stole which she had inherited from my grandma. He had the fur flung around his bare shoulders, and the rest of him was covered with mud. From head to foot. He was a wreck. So was the mink stole.

"But it's to keep *warm*," he protested.

"Your *clothes* are to keep you warm!" Mom shouted. "I don't know why you thought you should cover yourself with mud, of all things!"

73

"I think he thinks he's an Indian," I said.

That was reckless of me. I always forget that when Mom's mad at something, the next person who walks by makes her mad, too.

"I *am* an Indian," Jason said.

Mom turned on me. "Are you responsible for this?" she hollered.

"NO!" I screamed. "I'm not! Honest. In fact, I told him he *couldn't* be an Indian. So you can't pin this one on me."

"But I *can* be," Jason yelled. "Daddy said I can. I asked him, and he said I can be an Indian if I want."

I *knew* it. "*AHA!*" I said. "*AHA, AHA.* You see? I'm not the one who fills him with dumb ideas. So go yell at Dad, why don't you."

"Melissa Woodbury, you're about to get in serious trouble with me. You just go inside and start a warm tub for Jason."

"But..."

"*NOW,*" she yelled, snatching up the hose with one hand, and hauling Jason toward the middle of the yard with the other.

I went. Not that I minded filling the tub, but I thought Dad should do it. As it was, I was pretty sure he would get off scot-free.

Jason couldn't go right to sleep that night. I guess he's not so used to having people get mad at him as I am. Plus, he didn't like getting rinsed with the hose one bit. Mom hosed off the fur, too, which Dad told her was probably the wrong way to clean mink. It looked like something that had drowned.

"Don't worry about it, Squirt," I said in the dark. I could still hear him sniveling every once in a while.

"I'm not worried, Lissa. I'm just sad."

"Well, don't be sad then, okay?"

"Okay . . . But, Lissa?"

"Hmmm?"

"It didn't work."

"Yeah, I know," I said. "The trouble is that nobody can just decide to be an Indian, Jason. You either are one or you aren't."

"I know. But the *mud* didn't work. I got goose bumbles all over."

"Goose *bumps*. I'm sorry it didn't work, Jason."

"I guess it only works for real Indians, huh?"

"Probably," I said. "That's probably it."

He heaved a big sigh. "G'night, Lissa," he said.

"Good night, Squirt," I said. "Sweet dreams."

10

THE DAY BEFORE our projects were due, Mr. Shipley hung a sign-up sheet on the wall so that whoever wanted to give theirs first could. He said it would make more sense to do it that way because some people had lots of posters and stuff to bring in, and there wasn't any place to keep things until we gave our reports.

I was mainly relieved because that way I'd know exactly what day I had to give my report. I hate the suspense, for one thing. Sometimes if I think I'm about to be called on, I can't even concentrate on what other people are saying. I just sit there and worry about whether I'll do well or end up looking dumb. Also, I still wasn't quite finished with my project, so I knew that if I put my name way down on the list I'd have a little more time. We were going to give one or two reports a day, so I calculated nearly three weeks to get them all finished. I put my name third from last.

Katie said she didn't much care when she gave her report, so she ended up putting her name approximately in the middle. But Debra put hers right at the top. Naturally.

On the first day for giving reports, Debra showed up dressed in her best clothes. Well, maybe they weren't Debra's best clothes, but they would have been *my* best clothes. She looked like she was going to church or a party or something. I suppose she thought she had to look important because her project was that she had interviewed the mayor.

Everyone thought it was great. Or almost everyone. She had a photograph of the mayor, which he had autographed, and she even had a cassette tape of the interview, which she played parts of. She asked things like, "Tell me, what's it *really* like to be mayor?" And he'd give these inane answers like, "Well, to tell you the truth, it's really nice." I got the idea Debra was practicing to be Barbara Walters. Mostly she just stood there and raved about how important it was to be mayor, and how you had to be very responsible and everything. And she managed to squeeze in that she got the interview because her father "knew the mayor personally."

At question time, Zack stood up and said, "I've heard that the mayor only cares about people who want to build pinball and video arcades all over town. Could you tell us about that?" Debra just fumbled around for a minute and finally said, "Well, I didn't have time to ask him *every*thing. The mayor's very busy, you know."

"But that's *important*," Zack said. "There's been stuff about it in the papers. You should have asked him about that, instead of asking him if all mayors wore pin-striped suits."

Mr. Shipley interrupted and asked if anyone else had

any questions. Nobody did, so he thanked Debra and told her she'd done a nice job and could sit back down.

As she walked back to her seat, lots of people complimented her on how good her report was, and how neat it was to get an interview with the mayor. I didn't say anything, of course, because personally I thought it was a dumb report. Not that I'd have told her if I thought it was good. But I happen to know Zack's right about the mayor because my father has been ranting about what an idiot he is, and how he's going to ruin this town. Besides, it's not such a big deal to get an interview with the mayor, because when he's not busy being mayor he's at the used-car lot he owns, trying to drum up business. Anyone who wants to talk to him can just go there.

I figured, though, that even if other kids knew the mayor was an idiot, they wouldn't want to say so—at least the girls—because then Debra might get mad and not invite them into her club. I was thinking about that while Rob started his report (it was about public transportation), when it dawned on me that everyone already *was* in FUNCHY. Except for me and Katie and Bernice. Me for obvious reasons. I know Debra still can't stand me, even if she doesn't bother to act nasty anymore. And of course she wouldn't ask Katie, since Katie is my best friend and I'm sure Debra knows Katie wouldn't join without me. And then there's Bernice, who is still pining.

Knowing Debra, she's just going to let Bernice suffer a while longer. Possibly forever.

I thought Rob's report was pretty good. He ended up saying the transit system in this town is completely inadequate, because it's easier to get to San Francisco than it is to get around Westmont. I know he's right about that because every time I think about taking the bus, it doesn't go anywhere near where I want to go. I always end up walking or riding my bike. Mr. Shipley thought Rob's report was good, too, you could tell.

A few days later Joel gave his report. Everyone liked it because he had lots of pictures of all different kinds of fire engines, including some really old ones. And he told about this dog, a dalmation, that had been with this one fire company for over twenty years until it died and they buried it behind the firehouse. Plus, he brought in some printed pages to hand out to everyone, telling what you should do in case of a fire, and how to prevent them, and that smoke alarms are a good idea. He even gave out these stickers that you put on kids' bedroom windows so firemen can find the children quicker. I got two, and took them home for Jason's and my room. It seemed like a good idea to help out the firemen, even though our bedroom is so near to the ground I think I could just grab Jason and jump right out.

It was a couple of nights later, while we were having spaghetti for dinner, that Katie phoned. Most of dinner time Jason had been getting a lot of attention for having learned to say *wr* words, like *write* and *wring* and *wrong*. They always came out *wite* and *wing* and *wong* before, when they came out at all. Now Dad and Jason were making a lot of corny jokes about how Jason used to say "right wrong and wrong wrong," and now he can say "right right and wrong right." I guess if you're five years old, you'll laugh at anything.

I didn't really mind much, though. I was in a good mood and doing a superb job of twirling my spaghetti on my fork, when the phone rang.

"To what do I owe this honor?" I said. I always say that when Katie calls because she hates to make phone calls. She doesn't mind if someone calls her, but if she has to make the call she gets really nervous, even if it's just me.

"Well, I needed to talk to you," Katie said. "I mean I have something I need to ask you about."

"Okay," I said cheerfully, "ask away!"

"Well, it's about FUNCHY."

"Oh. Well, you can't ask *me* about that. Because I still haven't found out what they're about, if that's what you want to know."

"Not exactly," Katie said. "I mean . . . well, I guess I really wanted to *tell* you something and *then* ask you something."

"Yeah?" Something was starting to sound odd about the way Katie was talking, but I couldn't quite figure out what.

"It's . . . well, you know how after school in the coatroom Debra said she had something for me?"

"Oh, that," I said. "What was it, a special leaf for your tree report or something?" I was partly trying to crack a joke. But it didn't sound funny, and also as soon as I said it, I knew I was wrong.

"No. It was . . . Actually, she gave me an invitation to join FUNCHY."

"Oh," I said.

Of course I knew that in a second Katie was going to say that she'd told Debra she didn't want to join. Still, for some reason I suddenly felt lightheaded. I started to stare very intently at a loose thread on the cuff of my jeans.

"Umm . . . I was wondering," Katie said very slowly, ". . . what I wanted to ask . . . uh, how you'd feel if I, uh, joined?"

"Oh."

"I mean, would you mind?"

"Uh . . ."

" 'Cause if you'd mind, then I really wouldn't. Honest, I wouldn't, Lissa."

" . . . " I started to tug at the thread on my cuff.

"Lissa? . . . Are you there?"

"Yeah, I'm here." The thread was stubborn, but it started

80

to unravel. "You don't really want to join, of course. Do you?"

"Mmmm. Well, that's the thing. I was sort of thinking about it, if you wouldn't mind that is..."

"I guess that..." I got stuck. My voice sounded high-pitched and far away to me, and I wondered if it sounded that way to Katie. "Well...but *why*, Katie? Don't you..."

"See, it's just that I thought if you didn't mind I'd join, anyway. I mean, I know that you don't like Debra and all..." Katie's words were coming all in a rush, "but she's really not so bad sometimes. And she's been so nice to me lately. And to tell you the truth, I'm kind of tired of being left out. If you know what I mean. Anyhow, I think she'll probably ask you next. Pretty soon, I bet. It just stands to reason, right? And then we'd be together again as usual, right?"

"Katie..."

"Would you mind? I mean, I could tell you all about it and everything, while Debra's getting your invitation..."

It's amazing how fast you can unravel a hem if you really try.

"Katie. It's okay. Forget it. I mean, it's okay if you really want to join. I won't mind, really I won't." My whole cuff was undone, and I started picking at the fringe edge.

"Are you sure? Really?"

"Sure," I said. I didn't know who was talking anymore, but it definitely wasn't me. "Do whatever you want. I really won't mind. Only I have to get off the phone now, okay?"

"Lissa?"

"No, I have to go. But it's all right. I'll see you tomorrow, okay?"

I don't know if she answered or not, but I put down the receiver and stared at my cuff. It was a total wreck, and I couldn't figure out who had done it.

"Is something wrong, Lissa?" I could feel my mother's hand on my shoulder. "You're shaking, and look what you've done to your jeans..."

"I DIDN'T," I hollered. "And stop picking on me. You're always nagging me about something." I stood up. "You think Jason's so great, and he's *not*. So just quit being mean to me all the time!" I ran from the room.

A canopy bed would have been a real help, but since I didn't have one I just got way down under my covers. I didn't even bother with pj's, and when Mom brought Jason in to put him to bed, it sounded like they were on another planet.

Mostly I just wanted to sleep, but I was thinking at about ninety-five miles per hour and couldn't. I was imagining what it was going to be like at lunch tomorrow when Katie went over to the stump with the rest of the group. Should I just sit at our spot on the benches alone? Would Bernice suddenly decide we were best friends and come and eat with me? Would Katie decide I had warts? Would Debra sit and give me smug looks from her stump-throne—looks that would go around corners, just in case I happened to eat somewhere else?

I was reasonably certain that even if Debra didn't give me smug looks, she'd be *feeling* them. Katie probably wouldn't notice, since Katie seemed to have lost the ability to notice things about Debra. But I'd know.

I started making a list of possible ways to make enough money to go away to boarding school. That must be when I finally fell asleep...

11

I SOLVED my lunch problem the next day by simply not taking any lunch to school. There was no way I was going to sit on that bench alone, with that whole mob gathered around the stump, including Katie. So when lunch time came, I went into the library, sat on a cushion in the reading nook and stared at a book.

I was afraid Mrs. Ivers might chase me out. Or even worse, try to talk to me. She'd look at me with her weird eyes, and I'd get all creepy-feeling. But she didn't do either one. She just glanced at me once, and went on eating her lunch at her desk. Maybe it's the only time during the day she gets to herself, and she didn't feel like interrupting her lunch hour to bother with me. So I got to stare at my book and feel miserable in peace until the bell rang, and it was time for class again.

After school I left as quickly as possible. But Katie caught up with me before I got off the school grounds.

"Lissa, wait. Are you okay?"

"Yeah, I'm fine," I said. Hungry and lonely, but fine. It made perfect sense. "I see you got your pin," I said. Katie was wearing a FUNCHY pin on the neck of her blouse. It looked about five times as large to me as everyone else's, but of course it wasn't.

"Oh, yeah," she said. She blushed a little and stared at the ground.

I started staring at the ground, too. I couldn't think of anything to say next. Finally Katie mumbled, "It's not such a big deal."

"Oh," I said. "Well . . . so what's it about then? Now at least I can find out what FUNCHY's about." I tried to sound a little more cheerful.

Katie's face turned bright red, and she stared at the ground even harder. "I can't," she almost whispered.

"What?"

"I can't tell, Lissa. I had to swear. I'm sorry, truly, but I just can't."

That made me really mad. But Katie looked like she was about to cry, so I didn't quite want to start yelling at her or anything.

We both just stood there for a couple of minutes more, not saying a word. I stared at the ground. Then I stared at a bush. I gazed off in the direction of home for a bit, and then turned back toward Katie.

That's when it hit me. I suddenly realized I wanted to be in FUNCHY Club. All at once, I had this overwhelming feeling of wanting to be in it more than anything in the world. Me, Lissa Woodbury, wanting to be in Debra Dobbins's dumb club. But I couldn't help it.

"Do you think she's going to invite me?" I asked.

"I don't know," Katie said.

"Well, maybe you could sort of suggest it or something, you know?"

"I already did," Katie said, "but I don't know. Debra says she doesn't want to because she thinks you'd spoil it. I told her you wouldn't, but that's what she thinks."

"Well, it's a lie. I wouldn't spoil anything. You know that. So maybe you could just keep working on it, huh?"

"I'm going to. Honest, Lissa, I'm really going to try. Okay?"

"Okay," I said. And try hard, I thought, because it's really important. Otherwise I'm going to have to spend every lunch time for the rest of my life hiding out in the library.

After that, Katie and I more or less avoided each other. Not that I was furious with her or anything, but I wasn't going to go following her around begging her to be my friend either. I hoped she really meant it about trying to get me into FUNCHY. But I also knew there wasn't much I could do about it one way or another. In the meantime, Mrs. Ivers seemed to be getting used to having me in the library.

My nook in the library was comfortable, but as a hiding place it turned out not to be that great.

I'd only been there for a few days when Mr. Shipley wandered through the library one lunch time and spotted me. He actually asked me why I wasn't outside eating with the rest of the kids, and I couldn't think of anything to say at first. Then I told him I was on a diet. It was kind of lame, and I'm not sure that he bought it. But then he crouched down next to me and said he was getting worried about me because I didn't seem to "mix in" with the other kids as much as I should, and was everything okay at home?

It annoyed me that he said that, and I just stared at him thinking, Boy, are you dumb. There's this big illegal club here, and you think I'm *trying* to be a misfit. Why don't you ask Debra why I don't eat lunch with the other kids?

Finally, I said, "Everything's fine at home," and went back to my book.

He stood up then and said, "Well, if you ever want to talk to someone, I'm always available."

Fat chance. Of course I *could* go talk to him and tell him all about Debra and FUNCHY and a few other things besides. And then I could lie awake at night and wonder when Debra would have my house fire-bombed. I decided I had enough trouble as it was.

Then, as if a visit from Mr. Shipley wasn't enough, Zack tracked me down in the library a couple of days later.

"Oh, there you are," he said. "I've been looking for you the past ten minutes."

"That long, huh," I said. I didn't want to give him any openings because, knowing Zack, he was going to say something I didn't like. His nostrils were twitching already.

"No problem," he said. "I can spare the time. What are you doing here, anyway?"

"Improving my mind. So maybe you should leave so I can keep at it."

"Oh, I'm not staying," he said. "I just dropped by to compliment you on your good sense."

I thought maybe if I pretended to be deaf he'd just leave. So I stared at my book and didn't say anything.

"I mean it's not everyone who exhibits such wisdom," he went on. "In fact, you're the only one."

I sighed and closed the book. "Okay, Zack. What did I do this time?"

"Why, burned your invitation, of course. You *did* burn it, didn't you?"

"What invitation?" I asked, about a split second before I realized what he was talking about.

"Your invitation to FUNCHY, naturally. I knew I could count on you, Lissa. There had to be one person left around here who would decline the privilege of being Debbie Dobbins's flunky."

I couldn't tell if he really thought I'd had an invitation or not, and for some reason I was embarrassed to admit I really wanted one—that if I ever got one I'd probably *frame* it, not burn it. So I just said, "I'm really busy, Zack. So if you're finished, you can leave now."

"Oh, I can't stay, anyway. But I just wanted to let you know that I admire your stance. Especially now that you're the only girl not in that nitwit club."

"Except Bernice," I said. "Don't forget her. Maybe you should go admire her, too."

"Oh, no, I can't do that. Bernice *is* in, hadn't you heard? At least she got her invitation today, and I daresay she'll accept. She's ecstatic."

"Impossible! Zack Brady, you're making that up. She *can't* be in FUNCHY. Debra can't stand Bernice. Nobody can stand her. She's the most unpopular person in the whole class."

"Is she?" Zack said, scratching his head and pretending to look puzzled. "Gee, I thought that was me. Well, if it *wasn't* me, it is now. 'Cause ol' Bernice has just joined the ranks of the popular."

I blinked. He wasn't kidding. I could tell.

And I also knew he was wrong: Zack wasn't the most unpopular kid in the class, *I* was. This made it official. Signed, sealed and delivered. The Official Class Creep.

Congratulations, I said to myself. Welcome to total geek-dom. Good going, Lissa.

I didn't want to face going back to class. I thought of just leaving the library and walking home. But the way things had been going lately, I'd be sure to get caught. Then I'd be a truant, too. A truant and a geek. I knew I couldn't handle that, so I decided to go straight to my desk and let everyone have their big laugh.

Fortunately, though, nobody seemed to notice me. It would have been hard for anyone to notice anything that afternoon except Bernice Wilkins. I've never seen anyone so happy in my life. She was showing her invitation around to anyone who would look at it (I do wish Debra would quit using my four-color pen), and gushing about what she was going to wear the next day, and how happy her mother would be.

I was glad to be invisible when the bell rang so I could dash out first without being noticed. I've been doing a lot of that lately—being the first one out. Maybe I should be a professional escape artist when I grow up, like Houdini or someone. I wonder if Houdini was the most unpopular person in his whole class, too?

When you think about it, it was less than two months ago that I was unhappy about getting only eight Valentine's cards. It's a good thing Valentine's Day isn't in April. I'd get a minus twenty-seven.

As soon as I got home, I rushed into my room and started scrounging through my bottom drawer for my Lethal Lollipop. That's a lollipop I had when I got strep throat, back when I was about seven years old. I got too sick at the time to care much about it, so I hardly sucked on it. Then, when I got well and wanted it, my mom said I had to throw it out because it was probably covered with strep-throat germs. But I got this inspiration that maybe some-day I would *want* to be sick, so I'd miss the dentist or something, and so I saved it. For years, it's been wrapped in a piece of waxed paper in my bottom drawer. Lots of times I thought of using it, but somehow nothing ever quite seemed worth the agony of strep throat.

Until now, that is. There was no way I was going to go to school the next day and watch Bernice be delirious with joy over her initiation. Or have people make fun of me. Or, worse yet, feel sorry for me. How humiliating. I *had* to get out of going to school, and getting sick was the only way I could think of.

I sucked like mad on the lollipop. Part of the wrapper had peeled away while it was in the drawer, and it was a little dusty. But I couldn't risk rinsing it and sending all those germs down the drain.

When it was done, I tossed the stick in the trash can, put on my nightie, got a stack of my favorite books and piled them on the bed and climbed in to wait. That's where Mom found me when she got home from work.

"What's wrong?" she asked, looking concerned.

"I'm getting sick," I said. "I think I'm getting a sore throat. A really bad one."

Mom came over and put her hand on my forehead. That's always her first move, even if I only stub my toe. It drives me crazy.

"Well, you don't have a fever, Lissa. So why don't you just stay put until dinner time, and we'll see how you are then."

"Okay," I said. I intended to. I intended to stay put for at least twenty-four hours.

By the time dinner was ready, my throat still felt normal. And I was beginning to get worried. If I couldn't come down with a bona fide sore throat, I was going to have to fake it.

"Do you think you can eat?" Mom asked.

"I'll try," I said. I tried hard not to gobble. Since I'd been skipping lunch, I was always starved by dinner time. It was nearly impossible to eat slowly, much less languidly like a sick person would.

"I call that a good appetite," Dad said. "She doesn't look sick to me."

"Oh, but I *am*. It must be the fever or something—'feed a fever,' right? I think I'd better go lie down. And maybe you should keep Jason away from me, in case I'm contagious or something. In fact, probably you should all stay away from me. I wouldn't want the whole family to catch it." I shoved my chair under the table and beat it back to my room.

Later, after Mom had tucked Jason in bed, she came and felt my forehead again and started asking a lot of personal questions about my stomach, and whether I'd had any diarrhea, and what my throat felt like. I told her my throat felt like it had a thousand pins in it, but the rest of me was okay. She took my temperature, which was unfortunately normal, even though I tried to imagine my mouth was a furnace, heating the thermometer up to 104°.

Then she got a flashlight and looked in my throat and made me say, "Ahh."

"It looks healthy in there to me, Lissa."

"But it doesn't *feel* healthy. Are you sure my tonsils aren't red?"

"I'm sure."

"No little white spots on them?"

"Nope."

"Well, there will be," I said. "Just wait. By morning it's going to be really gross in there. You'd better call the school first thing and tell them I won't be there."

Mom got silent. It's different from simply not talking. She has this way of getting super silent and staring at you with her expression locked in neutral. I hate that look. She always uses it just before she lowers the boom.

90

"Melissa, there is nothing wrong with you," she said in a very level voice, "and you are *not* staying home from school tomorrow. So do you want to tell me what this is all about?"

"No! And I *can't* go to school, really I can't. And I *am* sick. Or at least I *will* be if I have to go to school tomorrow. So can't you let me stay home? Just this once? I promise I'll get well soon. Honest. Just let me stay home this one time..." All of a sudden I felt exhausted and realized I was crying. My nose was running—all over Mom's shirt.

Mom hugged me for a long time, which felt good. I haven't been as interested in hugs these days as I used to be, but I guess there are times you really need them. After she had patted me on the back about a million times, and finally fished a Kleenex out of her pocket for me, she said maybe she could *consider* letting me stay home. But she'd have to know the whole story first, so she could decide if it made sense.

So I told her everything. About how Jason spoiled the cheerleaders and Debra thinks he's retarded, and that Debra really hates me now, and even Katie isn't my friend anymore. And that I'm the biggest drip in the class now, even worse than Bernice, and that I just couldn't go to school tomorrow because I knew I'd never be able to pretend I didn't care that I was the only one not in FUNCHY.

Mom got pretty mad. She said she thought the whole thing was outrageous. She said she had a good mind to march right up to school the next day and put a stop to FUNCHY.

That made me practically hysterical. I told her it would just make everyone hate me worse, and that I could work it out myself. But I just needed one day off first.

Finally she said she'd go talk it over with Dad. I stayed there, sitting up, for the longest time, listening to them debate back and forth. I could hear their voices rise and fall, but I couldn't hear the words. My Kleenex was in little shreds by the time Mom got back.

"Once," she said. She sounded stern. "Just this one time you may stay home, and never again. Your father thinks it's setting a bad precedent, so you have to understand it's just this once."

"Thanks, Mom. Really, thanks. Once is enough."

"This means you have to work things out when you get back to school Monday. You can't run away from your problems, you know. And if you can't work them out, we'll go to school and work them out for you. But whatever happens, you can't stay home again. Understand?"

"I won't ask to," I said. "But, thanks, Mom. I really needed it this time, honest I did."

"I know you did," she said, sounding a little less severe. She tucked in all the sides of my bed, which she usually only does for Jason, and then she got my old teddy bear off the shelf and stuffed it in my arms. I started to giggle. I was already clutching my rabbit.

"Well, I suppose we can look at it this way," she said, starting to chuckle herself, "health is health. Tomorrow you're having a *mental* health day."

"Thanks," I said, laughing. I felt so relieved.

"You're welcome," she said, and turned out the light.

12

I SPENT MOST of the weekend just reading and resting and doing nothing. I didn't even get dressed on Friday and Saturday, and I kept expecting Mom and Dad to crab at me about it, but they didn't.

On Saturday, I finished my Indian project. I was all done, anyway, except for organizing what I was going to say, so I got a bunch of index cards and wrote down the main categories of stuff I wanted to tell about. I was going to be the first person on Wednesday to give my report, and I didn't want to be all worried about it on Tuesday night like I usually am if I'm not ready.

I didn't come up with any brilliant ideas about how to handle my problem of being Official Class Creep, because to tell you the truth I didn't spend much time thinking about it. There didn't seem to be anything *to* think about, mostly, except that I was going to have to get used to it. Bernice had been used to it for years, after all, so I supposed I could adjust.

The thing was, I didn't want to get all desperate-acting like Bernice always was, so I decided I'd just keep hanging around in the library and ignore the kids in class. Unless of course someone decided to be nice to me. Then I'd be nice back.

Monday morning I kept my attention riveted on my schoolwork. It dawned on me that if I kept this up I'd end up with the best grades in class, all because nobody liked me. That struck me as kind of funny when I thought about what a crummy excuse it was for getting good grades. That must be what Dad means when he says "every cloud has a silver lining."

Then, when I got to the library, I found a book propped against my favorite cushion in the reading nook, with a note clipped to it:

Dear Lissa,
  This is a new book, and I thought you might like first crack at it. I think you'll enjoy it.
                                          —T. Ivers

It turned out to be my favorite kind, a mystery with a girl as the heroine. So that made two silver linings on one day.

In the afternoon, I made the mistake of breaking my be-studious rule and glanced over at Debra. I instantly regretted it. She was looking right at me, with the world's most smug expression on her face. She must have practiced it in the mirror all weekend. On Tuesday, I didn't give her the opportunity to use it again.

I washed my hair on Tuesday night and put out some

decent clothes for the next day—my beige cords that don't have any rips in them yet, and my light blue velour top. I didn't want to get all dressed up to give my report like Debra had, but I also didn't want people to be staring at me thinking about what a wreck I looked, instead of paying attention to my report.

I packed up all the loose and fragile things—the Indians and baskets and stuff—in a couple of shoe boxes, with tissue paper around them. Then the next morning, Dad gave me a ride to school early, and carried the base for the village into the class for me. I had it all set up on the display table and was in my seat reading before anyone else got to class. Some people went and looked at it before we had Morning Meeting, and someone even said they thought it was "neat." I figured they didn't know it was mine.

My report went great! I wasn't even nervous, probably because I couldn't think about how everyone hates me and give my report at the same time. I just took a look at the top index card in my pile, and started talking.

I told all about what Westmont used to look like before it was Westmont, and how there were tons of all different kinds of animals and plants for the Ohlones to use for food. And about how they went hunting, and gathered acorns and seeds and berries, and went fishing and dug for clams. I told about how the men used to go in "sweat houses," and how the women wove beautiful baskets, and that everyone used to take baths in the creek, the same creek that's down next to Hanley Park.

I told about how the Indians thought it was more important to share than it was to get rich and how they thought getting along with people was more important than being very powerful. And I told about how they thought that everything in the whole world was alive in a way, even rocks and spears and things, so that they treated everything very respectfully. Like they wouldn't want to mistreat one of their tools, or it might stop working for them. And if they were mean to a tree, it might not give them many acorns. So they were nice to the whole world.

There were so many things to tell that I lost track of how long I was talking until Debra waved her hand and said, "Mr. Shipley, she's going way over her time..." But it must have been okay, because Mr. Shipley just said, "Shhh," and I went ahead and finished the report. I told about how the Indians had been killed off, first by germs, and later, when the American settlers came from the east, by starvation and murder. When I got to the card where I'd written THE END, I just said, "And that's the end, unless there are questions."

Nobody raised their hands, so I started to go sit down. But then Mr. Shipley began clapping, then Zack started to clap, and then Joel and even Katie and a bunch of other people. In a second it seemed like everyone was clapping. I must have just stood there looking dumbfounded. No one had ever clapped for a report before.

Mr. Shipley asked me to explain some more about how Indians from different villages and tribes traded and got married and things, even when they spoke different languages and sometimes couldn't understand each other. After I explained that, he asked me how I'd gotten interested in the Ohlones. So I ended up telling about how Joel and I had discovered the shells while we were digging by the creek, and what happened after that. I was afraid that Joel would be mad that I let the whole class know we hang together during the summer. But instead he started grinning, so it must have been okay.

The next thing really surprised me. Mr. Shipley said he was going to mention my report to the sixth-grade teacher, and that he was pretty sure she'd be interested in having me come give it to her class, too, and would I be willing to do that?

"Sure!" I said. "I'd love it. I mean, I'd be glad to." Wow. He'd never done anything like that before, so he must have thought it was fabulous. I looked at Joel because I thought he'd be grinning even more. But he was staring at his thumbs, and he didn't look all that happy anymore.

"Uh, Mr. Shipley," I said, "I was just wondering. It's an awful lot of stuff for me to cart around to the other classroom, so would it be okay if I had Joel help give the report next time? If he wants to, that is? Anyway, there wouldn't even *be* a report if Joel hadn't done all that digging with me..." I was talking and checking out Joel at the same time, since I hadn't asked first if he'd want to.

He wanted to. "Great!" he said. "And I have something else I can bring in that I found last week. I'd be glad to help, sure!"

Mr. Shipley said, "Fine" and that he'd make the arrangements and let us know what day.

I was in such a good mood that when I went to the library at lunch time I forgot to feel like an exile. It seemed like a natural and happy place to spend my time. I almost went up to Mrs. Ivers and told her about my report. But then I realized it would be breaking our unspoken agreement about how I didn't bother her and she didn't chase me out. So instead, I just plopped down in my spot and read the book she'd left for me on Monday, and was happy quietly.

I finished it before the bell rang, and I wrote Mrs. Ivers a note:

Dear Mrs. Ivers,
    Thanks for letting me read this first. I did like it!

97

You were right! Anytime you want to leave another, it's OK.

Your friend,
Lissa Woodbury

P.S. I gave a report in social studies today. It was about the Ohlone Indians. Have you heard of them?

I left the note sticking out of the top of the book, and slipped it onto Mrs. Ivers' desk as I left. Maybe tomorrow there'd be another book waiting for me. Maybe Mrs. Ivers and I would get to be good friends.

When I got back to our room, there was a big crowd of people around the display table in front of the room where my village was. There was a lot of commotion, and I thought, Hey, my village is really a success.

Only it wasn't that kind of commotion, because in a second I could hear Zack above the other voices, and he was having a total fit.

"It's outrageous," he was yelling. "Somebody ought to call the police. Take fingerprints or something! Catch the perpetrator!"

Nobody was telling him to shut up, which was odd. Mr. Shipley was standing right there letting Zack rant and rave, and not doing a thing about it. In fact Mr. Shipley looked like he wanted to rant and rave, too, but not at Zack.

Mr. Shipley spotted me and started my way. I didn't know what I'd done wrong—he looked awfully mad. I wanted to run out of the room.

"I'm sorry, Lissa..." he began

"Sorry what?" I said... Oh, no. My village.

"If they get away with this, I'm *quitting* this stupid school for good," Zack shouted. "People get away with doing a lot of pretty smelly things in this class, and someone had better put a stop to it!"

I pushed my way through to the table and looked at my village. I have a policy against crying in school. I haven't done it since I fell down the steps and split my chin open in first grade, and I wasn't going to start now. So I took lots of deep breaths, very slowly.

My Indians were all destroyed. All thirteen of them. All of them had their heads broken off, and some had arms or legs broken off, too. Three were completely crumbled. I picked up the pieces to my special lady, the one I'd made the day Jason covered himself with mud. Policy or no policy, someone's tears were getting all over her, and I was pretty sure they were mine.

"I'm sorry," Mr. Shipley was saying. "Lissa, I can't imagine who would do such a thing, but I'm going to try to find out..."

I could. I could imagine quite well. I looked around to see where Debra was. She was sitting at her desk, just staring out the window.

"...meanwhile, the important thing," he went on, "is to see what we can do to help you salvage some of this."

I felt like he was talking to me from the end of a long, hollow tube. The important thing to me *wasn't* to "salvage some of this" right now. The important thing to me was that my Indians were ruined, and I knew who had done it.

"I know who did it," I said, looking at Debra. Debra just kept staring out the window. It was suddenly very quiet in the room. Because of course you couldn't hear the heads swivel back and forth as people looked at me, then at Debra, and back. I could even hear the birds singing outside. It seemed strange for them to be singing when all my Indians were dead.

"Lissa?" Mr. Shipley looked at me. I looked back at him. We stood like that, staring at each other, for a few seconds.

Or a few years. Then it came to me that he didn't look like a movie star at all. Not one bit.

"But of course I can't actually *prove* who did it," I said. My face felt hot, and my nose was running all the way to my mouth. "So you're right, maybe the thing is to see what I can salvage."

I got the shoe boxes and started wrapping the pieces up in tissue paper. Joel helped, though I didn't notice him enough to feel glad about it. Zack had Mr. Shipley by the elbow, going on at him about how there were a few things Mr. Shipley should get wise to.

I didn't care about it. Right that minute I didn't care about anything.

13

THERE OUGHT to be an award for acting weird. I could have spent the rest of the day giving them out to people.

When I got home I put the shoe box on the dining table and took the lid off. Then I went to the freezer and helped myself to an enormous bowl of mint-chip ice cream. Most days I wouldn't dare do that. We're only supposed to eat nutritious snacks after school. But I figured that when Mom saw my wrecked Indians, she'd feel too sorry for me to holler about ice cream.

As soon as I'd finished, Mom walked in the door. I started to tell her about my day, but she interrupted me right away and said that Mr. Shipley had phoned her at work and told her "all about it."

I don't know what it was he told her, but I'm not sure

it was about me. I kept waiting for the sympathy she was going to give me about how awful things were, but it never came. Mom was too busy bubbling over with enthusiasm about what a great teacher Mr. Shipley is, and how he's "so concerned," and "so involved" and everything. Somehow he had managed to really knock her out.

"And he said your report was *quite* exceptional," she sparkled.

"Yeah, I guess he liked it," I said.

"He said you've got the makings of a first-rate social scientist. Your father will be so proud!" This was delivered with a hug.

"Thanks," I said. Of course, I really had archaeology in mind. But nobody was asking me.

"That's the mark of a truly excellent teacher, Lissa—to be able to recognize talent like that. You're lucky to have him."

"I guess so," I said. I was tempted to mention a couple of not-so-lucky things about having Mr. Shipley, but I thought, Why spoil her mood?

"So tell me, what would you like for dinner? Tacos? It's your choice. Something you'd really like, as a special treat."

"How about fresh crab?" I said. Not that I'd touch the stuff, but I wanted to check to see if she was still rational.

"Good heavens, Lissa! We can't afford crab. You know that."

"I'll have tacos then," I said. Might as well take what you can get.

She never even looked at my Indians. Not once. I picked up my shoe box and went into my room.

I was sitting on the floor working up a fresh wad of clay and trying to remember exactly what the crumbled Indians had looked like when Mom came in looking puzzled.

102

"Lissa, there's someone at the door who wants to talk to you. It's that strange kid, Brady somebody."

"Zack Brady! Good grief, what's he doing here?"

Zack was standing on the doorstep, looking both disheveled and overjoyed.

"What are you *doing* here?" I asked.

"Oh, well, it wasn't that hard," he said. "It's actually only a mile and three-eighths. I clocked it on the odometer on my bike. And most of it's downhill."

"Not *how*," I said. *"Why?"*

"Ah. I'm glad you asked that," he said. His nostrils were starting to twitch, and I began to get suspicious. I hoped he hadn't come all the way to my house just to make some lame joke.

"Actually, I have a present for you." He started to unzip his windbreaker. "I would have been here sooner, only I had to go home first and wrap it." He pulled out a small, brown paper bag.

"You had to go home to wrap it in that?"

"No, dummy, the wrapping's inside."

I pulled the bag open. Inside was a small, cylindrical-shaped gift, wrapped in paper with little hearts all over it. A red ribbon was at each end. It really threw me. Did this mean Zack was in love with me or something? I couldn't think of anything to say.

"Don't mind the paper," he said. "It was the only thing I could find." All of a sudden he reads minds, too, I thought. "Anyway," he went on, "I didn't give you a Valentine's card, so I thought it would make up..."

"You and about fifty other people," I said, tearing it open.

It was my pen. My four-color pen. It looked sort of beat up, but I knew it was mine.

"Zack! It's my pen. How did you..."

His nostrils were wiggling at about a hundred miles a

second. "I thought you might like it," he said. Then he burst out laughing. "Okay, so I *knew* you'd like it. Ain't it great?"

"I don't believe it! But how did you get it?"

"Oh," he said, trying to pull himself together. "Ahem. Well, you see . . ." He tried to manage a straight face. "Well, I'm sorry, but I can't tell you that, Lissa."

"*Zack*, tell me! Ohmigod . . . You stole it."

"Unfortunately, I can't divulge that information," he said. "It would make you an accessory, you see." I never saw Zack enjoy himself so much.

I didn't know whether to laugh, or hug him or just be astonished, which I already was.

"You'll never get away with it," I said. "I mean, who do you think you are?"

"I think I'm the Lone Ranger," he said, "but don't tell my parents. They'll have me locked up. See you tomorrow."

"Hey, wait!" I called. But he got on his BMX and pedaled off.

It was the first time I ever saw Zack leave before someone told him to go away.

"What did Zack want?" Mom asked.

"Well . . . he got my four-colored pen back for me," I said, showing it to her.

"Oh, now nice. Only I didn't realize it was lost."

"It wasn't," I said. "Or, that is, it was *missing*, not exactly lost . . ." I was beginning to lose the capacity to explain things, but luckily it didn't seem to matter. My mother was too busy making a mess of the kitchen to be interested in a mere pen.

The next person to show up was Joel, though at least he was expected. During school, he had offered to help me make my Indians over, so I was mainly pleased that he actually came.

"I brought glue," he said. "I thought maybe some of the ones that just had a part or two broken off could be glued."

"You can try if you want to. But the only thing I can ever get glue to work on is paper. Even then it doesn't always stick."

"This will work, don't worry. I was using it on a model spaceship one day and got a drop on the floor. Then I kneeled on it without noticing. There's still a little piece of blue material from my jeans stuck to the floor. Nobody can get it off."

I wasn't sure it would work as well on clay, but after a while five Indians were repaired, and Joel took a hunk of clay and started working on a replacement Indian. I was relieved we wouldn't have to make them all from scratch. And it was nice to have Joel there, to feel like we were still friends.

I was tempted to tell him about how Zack brought back my pen, and that I was pretty sure he had swiped it. But I wasn't sure I could trust Joel that much. If he was so crazy about Debra, he just might decide to tell her.

"You know," I said after a while, "if you want Debra to like you, you'd better not tell her you were helping me with these Indians." I was working on an Indian woman, and I glanced at Joel out of the corner of my eye. He turned red.

Maybe I shouldn't have said that about Debra, but I didn't care. "Don't blame me," I said. "Everyone has figured out you like her. It's no big secret anymore." Not to rub it in or anything, but I thought, Now that we're doing this project together I might as well be honest, right?

Joel's red turned a slightly deeper shade. But he just kept staring at the Indian he was making as though he hadn't heard me.

105

Okay, I thought, so be that way. We both worked in silence for a few minutes. I noticed that the Indian Joel was working on had developed knobby knees, and I wondered if I should mention it. Then I heard Joel, barely audible, say, "She's not so great."

"What?"

"Debra. She's not so great."

"Well, I know *that*," I said. "But I thought..."

"Some people *think* I like her," he interrupted, "but I don't really. I mean she has pretty hair and everything. But if you take a good look at her, you'll notice she has a face like a Cabbage Patch doll."

I roared. I laughed so hard I rolled on the floor and nearly squashed a fresh Indian.

"It's true," I gasped. "It's true, and I never thought of it that way."

"Well, I didn't expect it to crack you up," Joel said. He sounded gruff, but he looked pleased. "Anyway," he said, "I'd rather not talk about Debra."

"Whatever you say, Joel." I struggled to compose myself. "So let's talk about something else. What do you want to talk about?"

"As a matter of fact, this," he said, reaching in his back pocket.

He hauled out a small piece of ivory. It was about four inches long, oval shaped and covered with little, carved geometric designs. "I found it in the shell mound," he said. "I'm sure it's something that belonged to the Ohlones, only I don't know what it is."

"Wow," I said, utterly composed now.

"Yeah, it's pretty neat, huh? I called the archaeology department of the community college, and they said if I bring it in they'll help me figure out what it's supposed to be for. They said maybe it was an ornament—like jewelry—because of the carvings. But they have to see it before they can say for sure."

I turned it over in my hand. Knowing it was from the shell mound made it seem like the most special thing I had ever touched. Someone had carved it, probably thousands of years ago, and it had been left there at the creek by Hanley Park. I couldn't believe I was holding it.

"Wow," I said again. I didn't worry that I couldn't think of something smart to say.

"It's what I told Mr. Shipley I might bring in," he said. "Only I'm giving it to you. You'll have to be the one who brings it in. It's a present."

"Oh, Joel, are you sure? It's so beautiful. Are you sure you want to give it away?"

"I wouldn't give it to anyone but you," he said. "I mean, who else would care? But, yeah, I want to give it to you. I thought you'd like it even more than I do."

"I *love* it, Joel."

"There, you see? I was right."

I don't know how he did that, how he gave it to me. I know if *I* had found it I wouldn't want to give it to anyone. I turned it over and over in my palm, feeling the lines of all the carvings.

It must have been a long time before I remembered how to talk, then it just popped out. "Joel! You want to hear something hysterical? Guess what Zack did. Or, what I *think* he did..."

First I have a mother who doesn't notice that I'm devastated. Then two boys bring me presents, or sort-of presents. Then my father comes home and launches into a long debate with my mother about whether I should be a social scientist or an art critic. Neither of them noticed that I was nearby, hanging around, ready to tell them what *I* thought, in case anyone cared.

And Jason. Poor Jason. He turned on the TV and watched cartoons, and nobody came and got mad and turned it off. He probably thought his whole family had been replaced by clones. The first time I heard anyone speak to him was during dinner, when Dad said, "Hey, Jason, how do you like your taco?"

"Great!" Jason said, and beamed. He looked genuinely happy. Maybe a family of clones was just what he needed.

I was feeling pretty worn out by then, but Mom and Dad were still so caught up in their debate about my glorious future that I knew it wouldn't be too hard to get excused from the table.

"May I be excused?" I asked. Nobody answered. Then the phone rang. "To answer the phone," I said, and excused myself. Good thing it wasn't a fire alarm.

"Hi, it's Katie."

"Oh, hi," I said. I tried to sound nonchalant. Katie hadn't phoned me since she joined FUNCHY.

"How are you?" she said.

"Fine. I think." I hoped that would be her hardest question. It struck me as difficult when I had to answer it.

There was a pause. "I'm sorry about your Indians," she said.

"Yeah, me too," I said.

"Is there anything I can do to help?" Another tricky question. Talking to Katie was not as easy as it used to be.

I sighed. "I don't think so, but thanks."

"Well, in case I can..." she said.

"No, it's okay."

There was another silence. This one was longer. I was keeping track.

"I'm going to get you into that club," she blurted.

"Thanks," I said.

"No, I mean it. I'm going to get you in if it's the last thing I do."

"Thanks," I said again. This time *I* meant it. "But, Katie, it won't be easy. Debra hates my guts."

"I'll do it," she said.

"You don't mind if I ask *how,* do you?"

"Ask me later, after you get your invitation," she said.

At that rate, it struck me I'd never get a chance to ask. But I didn't say so.

"Anyway," Katie went on, "I've been thinking. It seems to me that even though I had to swear not to tell what FUNCHY Club is about, nobody said I couldn't tell you what we *do* there. So, if I tell you, nobody can complain. Right?"

"Sounds reasonable to me," I said. Actually, it didn't. Katie was saying a lot of things tonight that sounded very *un*reasonable, but I didn't want to insult her logic.

"So what *do* you do?" I asked.

"That's the thing," Katie said. "It's not such a big deal. Mostly we all sit around and talk. Only, Debra talks the most, of course. Mainly about herself. Oh, and she showed us her bra."

"Her *what?*"

Her bra."

"You're kidding. Debra has a bra?"

"Um-huh. And it's black."

"*BLACK,*" I screeched. "I don't believe it. I don't believe any of this."

"She did. She told us to all come in the girls' room, and she pulled her shirt up and there it was."

"But Debra doesn't *need* a bra. Not that I'm one to talk— I don't need one, either. But Debra needs one even less, if such a thing is possible."

"Yeah, I know," Katie started to snicker, "she doesn't. It was kind of funny, really, but of course I didn't laugh. Everyone was totally impressed, so I didn't say anything.

It was all made of lace—very elegant. Debra said it was the most expensive one in the store."

I'll bet it was. Debra certainly wouldn't show anyone a *cheap* bra. Of course, even if by some miracle Katie managed to get me into FUNCHY, I'd probably never get to see it. It seemed unlikely that she'd show it twice. Well, maybe she'd come up with something new. A spontaneous birthmark shaped like a unicorn or something. I wouldn't want to miss that.

"Promise you'll tell me the second you get your invitation," Katie said.

"Oh, I will, Katie. Absolutely." I wondered if Katie would ever hear from me again.

When I kissed Jason good night that night, I asked him if he had anything strange he wanted to say or do.

"No," he answered. Then after a bit he said, "Did I answer that right, Lissa?"

"*Just* right, Jason." Anyway, I guess it wasn't really his turn.

14

KATIE WAS so hyper the next day, she could have applied to NASA for a job orbiting in space. She kept looking over at me in class and flashing big grins. Then she waved crossed fingers at me, and kept squirming around in her seat. If she'd been any more energized, she could have launched herself. It started to get on my nerves.

I didn't especially want to get my hopes up that Katie could talk Debra into inviting me into FUNCHY, even though it was obvious Katie had hers up.

At lunch time, I just went into the library as usual. Mrs. Ivers had left another book for me on my cushion. It wasn't brand new, because it had been checked out once. But almost: I got absorbed in it right away, and was startled when the bell rang and I had to quit reading. It seemed like lunch time had been only ten minutes long.

As I headed out the library door, Bernice came panting in and managed to collide with me.

"I'm glad I found you," she said breathlessly. "Debra told me to bring this to you. It's very important." She stuffed a scruffy, ragged-looking piece of paper in my hand.

There it was:

Melissa Woodbury
Is Invited to Join
FUNCHY CLUB
Initiation Tomorrow
Nice Clothes If Possible
Bring Food to Share with Others
Signed,
Debra Dobbins,
Founder and President

It was written in pencil. I guess the Founder and President must have misplaced her four-color pen. I noticed that Debra didn't deliver it personally like she did everyone else's. I thought it was slightly insulting that she'd sent Bernice with it, of all people. Not that I was in a position to be choosy. At least I was in, which was amazing all by itself.

Katie grabbed me by the arm and whispered, "Well?" as I got back to the classroom.

"I got it," I said. Mr. Shipley was asking everyone to sit down, so I just had time to add, "I don't know how you did it, but, thanks..."

I glanced around for Debra, who spotted me and looked blank for a second. Then she gave me a rather sickly smile. I doubted I'd be her favorite club member. That's okay, I thought. Mainly I'd get to be with Katie, and I wouldn't be an outcast any longer. I hardly planned to suddenly be best friends with Debra.

All in all it was a pretty good afternoon. Mr. Shipley wandered by during math time and asked me how my Indians were coming, and whether I thought I'd have them reconstructed in time to give my report to the sixth grade in a week. I said that Joel was helping me, and I was sure we'd be done in time. I started to mention that Joel had made an Indian with knobby knees, then I realized Mr. Shipley probably wouldn't get it. I decided to save it for Katie.

I made a trip to the corner grocery store right after school. It's actually eight blocks away, but it's the nearest grocery store, and it's on a corner, so that's what we call it. I needed to get some "food to share with others." The food part took me by surprise, but then I'd never been told exactly *what* to expect at an initiation. I hoped there wouldn't be too many surprises, at least not unpleasant ones. No walking on hot coals in my bare feet or anything.

I had a certain amount of trouble figuring out what to get. Chips seemed too easy somehow, and sherbet would melt. Finally, I decided to make celery sticks stuffed with cream cheese and topped with sprouts. Then I worried that would be too dull, so I got some chopped walnuts to sprinkle on top, and some raisins. It's a good thing you only have to get initiated once, because it took more than five dollars to pay for it all, which was most of the allowance I had saved up.

Jason wanted to help make the celery sticks, and I said he could. When it comes to helping in the kitchen, Jason really shines. He's very methodical about doing exactly what's asked of him. He wouldn't touch the raisins, though. He said they looked like bugs. When we finished, I wrapped each celery stick in waxed paper, put them in a bag and

113

left them in the refrigerator overnight. We kept one separate for Jason.

For "nice clothes if possible" I laid out the same things I gave my Ohlone Indian report in. Debra would just have to put up with seeing me wear the same thing twice in one week.

I didn't expect to be nervous the next day about initiation, and I wasn't—not until lunch time actually came. Katie and I were walking toward the old stump together when I noticed I felt hot and sweaty. It was a sunny day, but there was an April wind blowing off a fog bank and the air was cool. So I suspected it was just me.

"I'm not going to have to do anything really bizarre, am I? Like make a speech, or spell everyone's name backward in less than five minutes?" I asked Katie.

"Don't be silly," she said. "All you really have to do is listen. Don't worry."

I hoped she was right. And I hoped the sprouts on my celery sticks hadn't wilted. I wiped the palms of my hands on my cords.

"Attention FUNCHY Club members," Debra intoned. "We have a new member today." She was sitting right on the stump, and everyone else was sitting on the ground in front of her, holding their lunch bags in their laps. Katie and I were standing—me because I thought I should, and Katie probably to give moral support. I thought I must look terrified, and tried to achieve a neutral face.

"We'll have the ceremony first, as usual, and then we'll eat," Debra went on. So far she hadn't looked at me. "And I'll start by reading the names of the present members." She hauled a small notebook out of her pocket and began to read the names of everyone who was there. I couldn't see the reason for that, but when you're new you don't always understand everything.

114

"And now for the rules," she said when she was done. "You have to promise not to tell anyone what this club is about. Do you promise that, Lissa?" She finally looked at me. I thought she had the fiercest eyes I'd ever seen.

"Yes," I said.

"You have to *swear. Do you swear?*"

Her gaze was petrifying. I had this awful feeling that if anyone found out the purpose of FUNCHY, we'd all be shipped to Siberia.

"Yes," I squeaked. "Er, ahem . . . *Yes.*"

"And that has to be a *solemn oath*," she said menacingly. "You understand there are penalties for anyone who breaks it."

"I understand."

"All right then. Here it is: FUNCHY stands for Fun Lunches. The purpose is for us all to eat together every single day, and we all *share* the lunches. Like a smorgasbord. Everybody brings something to share. So you can't bring any of your lousy peanut-butter-and-jelly sandwiches, Lissa. Got it?"

I nodded. I got it. I didn't much care for that reference to my sandwiches, but this was the wrong time to make waves. I waited for her to continue.

"Okay, so we can eat now," she said, and plopped down.

I just stood there, waiting for the rest.

"Wait," Katie said. "You forgot about the book."

"Oh, yeah," Debra said, and thrust her little notebook in my direction. "You can sign the membership book now."

I held the book for a minute and looked around at everyone. Something had been left out, I was sure of it. Or else I had missed something. I thought maybe someone else would mention it, but nobody did. Finally, I couldn't stand the suspense.

"Isn't there something else?" I asked.

Debra looked at me like I was crazy for a second. Then

a flash of recognition crossed her face and she smiled. "Oh, yes," she said, "the other purpose of FUNCHY is to talk."

"You get your pin at the *end* of lunch," Katie whispered reassuringly before she sat down.

I'd forgotten about the pin. I didn't *care* about the pin. I just wanted to know what else FUNCHY was about.

"Is that all, Debra?" I didn't want to be pushy, but...

"That's it," she said cheerfully, and dumped a bag of potato chips onto a paper plate in front of her.

"That's *it?*" I asked.

"Yeah."

"There's nothing else?"

"*No,*" she said. It was clear that I was beginning to annoy her.

"I just want to get this straight," I said. "You mean the big secret is that we share our lunches. And the only rule is we don't tell anyone the secret. That's the *whole thing?*"

She gave me a pained look, like I was an imbecile, too dim to catch on. "I *told* you, Lissa."

I stared at the membership book in my hand. This was it then. My name in this membership book, sharing my lunch every day and listening to Debra talk. Mainly about herself, as Katie had said. But why the big secret? Who would want to know? Who would *care?*

Katie was tugging at my pants leg to get me to sit down, but I couldn't move. I just kept staring at the membership book in my hand, and hoping the murky feeling in my head would disappear. Then I looked at Debra, who was now munching placidly on a potato chip. The Founder and President.

"You jerk," I said.

"What..."

"You jerk," I repeated more loudly. "You don't really expect me to join your stupid club just for the privilege of sharing my lunch and listening to *you* talk, do you?" The

116

murky feeling in my head had cleared. "That's the lamest excuse for a club I ever heard. Why don't you come right out and call it THE DEBRA DOBBINS IS GREAT CLUB? Starring Debra Dobbins. At least that would be honest.

"I quit," I said.

"Lissa..." I heard Katie say.

"No...No, I don't quit. I *decline*. I decline the big fat honor of your invitation. I'd throw up if I had to eat lunch with you every day..."

Debra seemed to be trying to say something, but her mouth just opened and closed, and a piece of potato chip fell out.

I retrieved my bag of celery sticks from the ground by Katie's knee. Then I stared again at the membership book I was holding in my other hand.

I opened my palm and watched as it fell to the ground with a slap.

"*Hey...*" Debra squealed.

"Drop dead, Debra," I said. "Just *drop dead*." Then I turned and walked away.

My old lunch bench was empty and looked inviting in the warm sunlight. I plunked myself down and dug into the bag of celery sticks. I bit into one, and gave a satisfying crunch. Not bad, I thought. The sprouts could have been fresher, but I was absolutely famished.

I decided there was something pleasant about eating by myself. I was all alone, but for some reason I didn't feel the least bit like an outcast. In fact, I felt like someone who'd just been released from jail. All the inmates were gathered at the stump.

Of course, tomorrow I might regret it. I might wake up in the morning and say, Ohmigod, what have I done? Suppose I'd had an attack of temporary insanity? They might lock me up in a cell. Right next to Zack's, no doubt.

I *could* just be in shock, I reasoned. I've heard about that—you can be in shock and forget to care about the most basic things.

But if I was crazy or in shock, would I feel so good? Somehow I doubted it.

I also doubted I'd be hiding out in the library at lunch time anymore. Mrs. Ivers would probably wonder what had happened to me. I'd have to drop in and talk to her, so she'd know it wasn't that I didn't appreciate her.

Even a starving person can eat only so many celery sticks. I quit after the eighth, leaned back against the sun-warmed wall and closed my eyes.

Bump. "Shove over," Katie said, "you're hogging all the room."

"Ha! We're all alone on a ten-foot bench, but for you I guess I can make some space," I said. "What are you doing here?"

"I came for my celery stick," she said, helping herself. "I really wish you'd been there. You should have seen Debra after you left. It was classic."

"I can imagine," I said.

"No, you'd have loved it. First she started in on you, of course—about how she knew you'd try to spoil it, and that you and I had been planning it all along. So naturally I said that wasn't true..."

"Oh, no! Oh, Katie, I'm sorry. I didn't mean to get you in trouble. It should have occurred to me she'd blame you."

"I didn't get in trouble," Katie said. "She wouldn't dare. Anyhow, she never got a chance, because I quit."

"You didn't!"

"Hmmm. And that wasn't the best of it. Next, Tina spoke up and said she thought the club should have a 'more serious purpose.' Then Debra started to argue with her, and Bernice just *had* to leap to Debra's defense. She said, 'But it *does* have a serious purpose. It's about Debra. And I agree, we should call it THE DEBRA DOBBINS IS GREAT CLUB.' People started laughing, and Debra looked like she wanted to kill Bernice."

"That's great," I laughed. "Oh, Katie, I'm so full."

"And *then*," she said, "and then Marla said she had to quit the club because her mother was sick of all the fancy lunch food. It was getting too expensive. And as soon as she said that, Cindy said the same thing. Then everyone started talking at once, and people were packing their lunches and making excuses for why they all had to quit. Except Bernice, of course. I have a feeling Bernice is going to be a lifetime member of FUNCHY."

I was holding my sides and trying not to laugh. My stomach hurt already.

"But, honest, Katie, I didn't know I was going to say all that stuff. It just popped out. I really thought I *wanted* to be in FUNCHY. Oh . . . and all the trouble you went to to get me invited!"

"What trouble? *That* was no trouble. It took me fifteen seconds flat!" Katie was really cracking up now.

"You're *joking*," I said. Did this mean that she had just never bothered to ask before? If that was true, I wasn't sure *how* I'd feel about Katie.

"No, I'm serious. It was a piece of cake. You see, I just took Debra aside and said that I'd seen her break your Indians, and if she didn't invite you into FUNCHY, I'd tell Mr. Shipley."

"You *saw* her? Oh, Katie, you should have told . . ."

"Of *course* I didn't see her," she laughed. "I was just *guessing*. But Debra doesn't know that."

"*Katie*," I screeched. Of all people . . . "That's blackmail!"

"Yeah, I know. You ought to try it sometime. It's more fun than you'd think." Katie was killing herself laughing.

Later I told Katie that in a way I wished she *had* seen Debra break my Indians. Part of me would have gotten a lot of satisfaction out of seeing Debra hanging by her thumbs, somewhere above the blackboard.

"Oh, terrific," she said. "I'm a blackmailer, and now you want to be a torturer. I'll tell you, Lissa, I'm not sure we're such a good influence on each other."

"Oh, Katie," I said, "I've really missed you. And I have so much to *tell* you. Like I made friends with Mrs. Ivers, and Joel brought me a present and made an Indian with knobby knees. Oh, and *Zack*. Wait till I tell you about Zack..."

Dad's car was in the driveway when I got home, so I knew he must have the flu or something. That's the only reason he comes home early from work. I went in the door quietly so I wouldn't wake him if he was sleeping.

I could have spared myself the trouble. Mom and Dad were in the kitchen, Dad polishing his shoes on the counter, and Mom frantically ironing one of his good shirts.

"Lissa, honey, guess what," Mom said. "Your father sold one of his paintings!"

"Really? Hey, wow! Congratulations." I gave Dad my most bone-crushing hug. "This has been a great day for the Woodburys," I said. "Including for me."

"Yeah, it's pretty exciting all right," he said.

"Which one did you sell?" I asked. "Are we going out to dinner to celebrate?"

"*Spring*," he said. "You know, the new one that you liked so much."

I looked at him to see if he was kidding, both about selling it and about how much I'd liked it. He didn't look like he was kidding.

"That's uh... *amazing*," I said. I tried to imagine who had bought it. Someone with a really ugly house, no doubt.

Or someone who wanted a painting to hang in his closet, some rich eccentric. "How much did you get? Are we going to be rich? Are we going to move so I can have a room of my own?" I didn't mention the canopy bed. First things first.

"Whoa," Dad said. "It wasn't that much. In fact, when you add up the canvas, the paint, the frame and the rental on the gallery space, our net profit was about thirty-five dollars. Then there are all those other paintings that have been losing money for years."

I was beginning to get the drift. "Not enough for a canopy bed, either, huh?"

"Not this time, kiddo. But cheer up," he said brightly, "it's a start!"

"So, where are we going for dinner?" I asked. I'd settle for McDonald's, at the rate things were going.

"We're not going out for dinner, Lissa. The man who bought the painting wants to meet the artist." He rubbed harder on his shoes. "It's an important occasion. I want to make the right impression."

It struck me that in his best suit and shiny shoes, he'd impress the guy as a banker. "Then I think you should wear your grubby blue jeans and the sweatshirt you wear when you're painting. And maybe carry a palette in one hand," I offered.

"Lissa," Mom said, "this is no time to be difficult. Why don't you go see if you can find Jason. I've lost track of him."

My parents. They sell a painting at a net loss of thousands of dollars, misplace Jason and don't bother to ask me how my day was. Then they say *I'm* difficult.

I found Jason sitting at the bottom of the back steps, pounding on the third step with his fist. Bam. Bam.

"Hiya, Jason!"

"Hi, Lissa." Bam. He didn't bother to look up.

"Would you like a celery stick? I have some left over."

"No thanks," he said. Bam.

"Would you like to hear about FUNCHY Club?" I asked, sitting on the top step. "I can tell you all about it." At least Jason would listen.

Bam. "Can I be a FUNCHY when I grow up?" he asked.

"Of course not, Squirt. Don't be silly."

"Then don't tell me, Lissa. I don't want to hear if I can't be one." Bam. Bam.

"But, *Jason...*" I said. Then I gave up. Maybe Jason was right. Maybe he was better off not knowing.

Bam. Bam, bam, bam.

"Jason, what *are* you doing?"

"Killing ants," he said. Bam.

I bent over for a closer look. Sure enough. He had intercepted a whole column of ants, and the body count was incredibly high.

"But, Jason, you're afraid of ants."

"Not anymore," he said happily. *BAM, BAM. BAM, BAM.*

"That's great," I laughed. "You're terrific, Jason, you know that? In fact, you're probably the most terrific person in this whole family..."

"I know, Lissa," he said with a giggle. Bam, bam. Bam.